NETWORK SECRET

A Mystery

NETWORK SECRET

A Mystery

The Sequel to
NETWORK OF DEATH

DANIEL HILL ZAFREN

Published by Time Treasures Books, Goose Creek, South Carolina

ISBN 13: 978-0-9833042-6-5

Printed in the United States of America

Cover and interior design by Susan Newman Design Inc.

List of earlier memorable works by the author:

In a World We Never Made (2001)
A Door Never Opened (2003) [sequel]
Shadow Selves (2005)
Network of Death (2006)
Not Lost – Just Not Found (2008)
Restless Beauty (2009)
Glimpses of Forgotten Dreams (2010)
Echo in the Heart (2011)
Double Hugs (2011)
Page Passage (2013)
Wish Winds (2014)
Unfinished Thinking (2015)
Vain Regrets (2016)

ONE

The stark reality had become a recurring nightmare whenever he could sleep. Even for a homicide detective who had been hardened to violent deaths over all of the career years, this one had been so personal, so close to his heart. He was finally on the verge of some sort of happiness with a woman he had discovered a mature love with, and he had retired to reap the benefits of that long overdue satisfaction when it abruptly ended. He was returning to the house where she lived and where he was staying with her, and when he opened the front door it was quiet in the house. She may have been at her job as a teacher late or she may have been upstairs taking a nap. He went upstairs and opened the bedroom door slowly. Even in the waning light his trained eye held the grotesque sight before him. Her lifeless body was spread out on the bed and massive amounts of blood had oozed out from the slashed neck. Scattered around on the floor were the broken pieces of turtle figurines.

It is said that time is the great healer. Yet, there are some wounds to the heart and spirit that no amount of time can salve. It had been five years since Alice had been taken so brutally from him, and every day for Howard Jensen was a form of reliving that episode and its devastating impact on his being. It did not help that the murder had gained national notoriety and a television documentary was made and aired on the event and its background. Apparently, North Vietnam as an act of revenge against a D.C. homicide detective who had agreed to help one of its commercial spies who committed treason and who had been able to kill a member of that nation's elite assassin squad, a person he loved was targeted instead of himself either as a warped form of punishment or as a show of power, or both. Discovery and destruction of the turtle collection was an ironic twist on the symbol of that group's identity. In the absence of sufficient tangible proof, unanswered international accusations was as far as justice got.

Howard and Alice had talked about getting married, but since they were not married at the time of her death Alice's assets did not pass to him. Money was not the interest to him. It was the well being of a promised loving future together with the rest and peace he craved.

He had stayed with Len Dressler and his family for awhile. Len was his partner as a homicide detective, and he had retired to become the sheriff in the same small town in which Howard was to be with Alice. Howard tried valiantly to sort out the reasons for everything and to ward off a growing feeling of doom. He had seen so many suicides during the detective days to know that was not a solution for him, although he had a greater understanding how such an act can be compelling.

Moving back to the District of Columbia seemed to be the only choice. He no longer had any interest in writing the mysteries with Len that they had planned. He rented a small apartment near Dupont Circle. Minimal furnishings were obtained at a local thrift shop. The Chief at the Homicide Bureau offered him his old job back, but Howard could not consider facing the grueling hours and unabating pressures to ever do that again. He had decided to give up police work even before the Network case. His meager savings would not carry him far so he took a job with an old acquaintance who had a gun shop on K Street. That acquaintance readily agreed to take on a man with extensive experience with firearms and who he knew was as honest as the day was long. Regular working hours at a busy store filled his days. The nights, however, were crowded with haunting memories and a longing that would never be satisfied.

Whenever he looked in the mirror he saw a decrepit old man, much older than his years. His fifty-seventh birthday had passed unnoticed and without meaning. He felt sorry for himself as he did for all people who existed as a form of autonomon just going through the motions without a heart-driven possibility of pleasure or pride. He had even gone beyond sensing pain as he felt nothing at all.

As in former days, he drank far too much coffee. There were no healthy or enjoyable meals. Fast food outlets were his source for food. He never had a cholesterol reading or any extensive blood testing, and he surmised that his organs were screaming for relief as were his muscles. At the root of it all was the abject feeling that he was living for no purpose at all. He had no way of knowing or even guessing this was about to change.

It was a slow morning at the gun store. Howard had just drained his fourth cup of coffee and was leaning on the front display case looking down at his image reflected in the glass top. He could plainly see the three-day stubble on his face and the top of the wrinkled shirt. A tip of the collar on one side pointed upwards as if it was seeking the sun or some other form of escape from the soiled garment. He should have taken a shower this morning but there was always the danger he would go down the drain with the water.

Still bent over, at first he thought someone was waving a bouquet of flowers before him. Then, it dawned on him that it was more likely expensive perfume. He looked up and saw a magnificent woman standing before him. A refined beauty encompassed a fetching and sophisticated form. The gray tweed suit was tailored to perfection and adorned a classic female shape. The voice was sultry and he should have remembered it because it was impossible to forget. "Howard?"

He straightened out his bent over form and looked into a set of large clear eyes. He sensed his lips quivering before the response was uttered. "So they tell me."

Sultriness has no equal and no bounds. "I am Grace Wharton."

One cannot totally escape from a trained and long-experienced past. The detective mode kicked in, and despite the time lapse and the major damage to his being, he recalled but could not clearly recognize that she was one of the Network women he had interviewed. She was one of the lucky ones and had not wound up dead. Both then and now, it was the voice that captured his attention. It was like a scintillating wind carrying him along in its current. "I remember you. You look different."

The smile was beguiling. "That is because I am different." A pause was for her not for him. "I need your help."

A stale and clouded mind could not obscure the outlandish request. *Who or why would anyone want him to do anything?* A blank stare was all he could muster.

Since he said nothing, she continued. Under other circumstances she might have turned around and left, but in her preset and orderly mind she had figured out this was the best way to proceed. "Can we go somewhere that is private so we can talk?"

Gruff meets sultry. "There is a lunch room in the back. The owner will watch the store."

"Lunch is a good idea. I noticed a deli a few doors down. I'll get us something to eat and drink. I remember you like your coffee black just as I do."

Before he could say anything she was out the door. He went to the restroom and splashed cold water on the weather and life-beaten face. His eyes barely focused on the image in the dirt streaked mirror. Again, the puzzling thought, *Why me?*

She returned with a bag and two large paper cup coffees. After placing the bag on the small table, she pulled out a roast beef sandwich and a corned beef sandwich. As she sat in a chair she handed him half of each sandwich without asking him. He sipped the hot coffee and took a bite of roast beef, real food for him. "Please forgive the way I look."

"You don't look any worse than the time you questioned me."

He was not sure she was trying to be humorous or just factual. Since there was no room for humor in his life he opted for factual. He just wanted her to keep on talking so he could bask for the moment in that sultry voice. "I remember you were afraid, and rightfully so."

"I was. I still am but now for a different reason. That is why I need your help."

Honesty will often usher in a form of bluntness. "I can't help myself. What makes you think I can help you?"

"I know all about the tragic event in your life and have followed the aftermath with much interest and sympathy. When I tell you of my life, you will understand. As you probably know, once the murderous group was caught and prosecuted, any and all actions against the individual women in the Network were dropped. All records were sealed. I could not go back to that kind of life. I moved back to North Carolina and took care of my invalid mother until she passed away. Using my Capitol Hill experience and contacts, I decided to run for a seat in the House of Representatives from the rural community I lived in. I won by a slim margin and have done well and plan to do even better in the future for my constituents and for the nation as a whole. I am up for re-election next year. All well and good until now. While nothing emerged about my past before and especially during the first campaign, now a blackmailer has surfaced and threatens to reveal my past unless I do not run again. No money has been asked for, but I sense this is just the tip of the iceberg. I know you and have a belief that I can trust you, and since you are officially out of the main stream I know you can find this blackmailer."

He already knew he would do it. That voice could persuade him to do any of her bidding and even vote for her although he did not live in her district. "There are professional private investigators who can do better than me."

"Perhaps. But, in my position, I might open more doors that way than I care to think about. Simple has worked for me, and this appears to be the way to go. I will pay you well and cover whatever expenses you incur."

"I'll try to help you, but that is all I can promise. I do know the world of crime, but the world of politics is beyond me."

She grabbed his rough-skinned hand. "Leave politics to me."

TWO

It must be the thrill of the chase that had given him an infusion of energy and purpose. Maybe it was just having a sultry benefactor. Maybe it was just the roast beef. Anyway, when he arrived back at the apartment, he stared at the hand-printed note that had been sent to her office in a plain envelope marked PRIVATE.

DO NOT RUN AGAIN OR ALL THE
WORLD WILL KNOW YOU ARE
A WHORE

Then he pulled out a large note pad and made two lists.

Those Who May Know But Who
Lack Credibility and Proof

*AWOLL members – presumably they are all in prison,
but it is possible some got away or were
never found, or contact could have been made
between an incarcerated member and one
on the outside.*

*North Korea officials.
Former Network ladies.
Clients at the conventions.*

Those Who Might Know and Have Credibility/Proof

*Special FBI Team that questioned
her at safe house.*

*Other FBI Members who investigated
computer records*

Network Officials, including recruiter

Chief, Homicide Bureau.

*Other detectives in the Bureau who may
have had access to records or parts
of the investigation at the time.*

Federal prosecutor

He shook his head. At this point no one should be ruled out. No doubt it was a large pool of suspects and he would need a big net and help. He spent an hour on the telephone with Len outlining the big picture and discussing the nuances. Len's computer skills and criminal diagnostic ability would be vital to narrow the hunt. In a way, it would be like old times when they worked on cases together. His wife, Joan, would probably not like it, but it was not as before when she could not be with him. The family unit was still together in the country.

Grace had given him a direct private telephone number that he could reach her whenever he needed to. She was pleased at the call and that he was already pursuing ideas. The questions were pointed and no less than she expected. "Do you remember the name of the woman who recruited you?"

The voice was spell-binding even on the telephone. "No. I am not even sure she gave it to me."

"Anything else you can recall about her or what she may have said?"

"All I noted at the time was that she was middle-aged, nicely dressed and articulate. She did not volunteer anything that she thought I need not know."

"Were there any Network ladies who knew you by name?"

"Not likely. We always used aliases at gatherings and any other meetings. I suppose it is possible one could remember my face, but I am fairly confident that my political pictures and current shots are a far cry from what I looked like then. Same story for any of the men I was with."

"Do you remember the FBI agent that questioned you?"

"It was a woman, a young woman. Farrell, or something close to that comes to mind."

"How about the D.C. detective who took you to the safe house?"

"I can't recall him giving me his name although he flashed his identification. He was short and pudgy. He didn't say much, and I did not expect or want him to say anything."

"Anyone else come to mind that you might suspect?"

"I have gone over and over possibilities since I received the note. All I get is a blank, except I wonder why it took this long. Do you think that might be important?"

"Could be. Clues can take any form. You do know that you can do a coup and just publicize it yourself somehow and then there would be no Network secret, nothing to blackmail you about?"

"That would be easy, wouldn't it? But, scandal is political suicide. The media would have a field day with it, and it would be too juicy for them to let it go. It's not an option."

"I just wanted to make sure that is the way you felt. I am afraid that unless we get lucky this might be a long haul. Try to get as much information from the blackmailer if he or she contacts you again. Since the note went to you at your office, either they do not know where you live or want you to think they do not know. If they do know the next contact may be there so that you will sense they know everything. Could be amateurish or very professional."

"I appreciate you doing this. I am confident you will help."

He sighed. "I wish I shared that sentiment."

THREE

While he would like to devote full attention to the investigation, it was best to work at the gun shop and just take time off as necessary. His activities would then seem to fit in with the devised scheme which was no longer true that he and Len were working on a mystery book on the Network case and they wanted to make it as authentic as possible.

He and Len discussed tactics and approach, and it was concluded to start with those who might have proof if push came to shove. Such a person would have greater confidence of success and stick with it if the going got tough.

Howard would tackle the D.C. Homicide Department first with a talk to the Chief and then the short and overweight detective who took Grace to the safe house. There was only one short and overweight detective there at the time so it did not take a Sherlock Holmes to figure that out.

The Chief probably thought Howard had reconsidered the offer to come back on board. He made it clear that was not his intention.

Chief Russell was a strange man, but his orderly efficiency made him a natural manager of people and affairs. He had been the Chief for fourteen years, and had been a detective there for twenty years before that. He was hardened to the job, and like Howard and many others there had been no room in his life for a wife and family.

Howard sat before the Chief's desk sipping the coffee that had been offered. "Len and I have decided to go ahead with a book on the Network case."

The Chief's voice was guttural, "Should be a good one and it would make even a better movie, as it has all of Hollywood's favorite ingredients, especially violence and sex. Why you want to do it is your business. I would stay as far away from it as I could."

"Makes good sense, but the way I figure it will be a form of self-punishment. No one can beat up on me better than me."

"You're either a genius or a fool."

"Let's leave that open-ended, but we both know the true answer."

The Chief shook his head. "What do you want from me?"

"I guess I just want to tap your memory for any details I have forgotten or never knew."

The Chief sighed, and Howard figured it was a combination of boredom and exasperation. Tired eyes squinted before the lips moved. "It's been more than five years and the records are sealed. They're supposedly in some vault in Virginia. Twenty lifetimes have passed since then. I won't be much help. Of course, I remember the case as it was a tough one and frustrating. In all my years I never saw one quite like it before or since. I remember we spent a lot of man hours and great expense with little result. But, as for details it is all one big blur now. I couldn't tell you a name, place or describe any person involved. Many cases have come through here since then. You were the closest to it day-to-day. If you or Len don't remember, it's gone. Nobody else will."

"Probably so. Do you mind if I talk to some of the guys?"

"Be my guest. Just don't be critical of the Department or any of us in the book."

"There's nothing to be critical about. A tough case got cracked. That's the bottom line."

The short overweight detective was Lars McDonald, brought up as a catholic but who rejected all religion except finding Satan in every criminal who walked the streets. He was tenacious in every case he worked, and he had been with the Department since he was twenty-seven and was now sixty-two. That's a lot of cases and a ton of Satans.

Lars was at his desk when Howard approached him. They exchanged a friendly greeting and Howard grabbed a cup of coffee from the pot in the corner. He sat by the desk. "How you been, Lars?"

"Better than you, I suppose. I had seen it all, or at least I thought I did, until what happened to you. I feel for you, my friend."

"I appreciate that. I am trying to emerge from the walking dead by writing a book with Len on the Network case. I won't keep you long but I have some gaps to fill in and you might be able to help."

"Fire away. That case was your baby so I wasn't close to much."

"Well, let's try it anyway." Howard drained the last of the coffee in the cup resting it on the corner of the desk. "As I recall, you accompanied one of the ladies to the safe house."

"Yeah, I remember that. Only probably because she was first class and one I would have dreamed about if I ever had a wet dream."

"Do you remember her name?"

"No. Not sure I was ever told it."

"Did you talk to her?"

"Look at me. What is a good-looking dish going to say to me.....or me to her? In fact, I am not sure she opened her mouth. I took her there, made sure we were not followed, and made sure she went inside. That's it, plain and simple."

"O.K. Thanks."

They shook hands. Lars offered, "If the book turns out to be a hit, I've had a bunch of cases over the years that would knock their socks off. Maybe we can work on one together."

"Maybe."

Howard telephoned Len to inform him that it appeared the D.C. Homicide Bureau was in the clear. Sure, there was a remote possibility that someone else at the Bureau could have overheard something or seen some of the records back then and even copied it, but Howard, sensing time was against that, dismissed it. He would never get this solved before the election if he got mired down in every possibility. His instinct told him he was after big game and not small potatoes.

The same report was given to Grace. He could have waited until he had something substantive to tell her, but he was addicted to that sultry voice. It may be the only thing keeping him going.

FOUR

Good ole Len, being the meticulous detective that he was, and because he never threw anything out which drove his wife, Joan, crazy, had buried in his notes on the case the name of the FBI agent who interviewed Grace. Victoria Farrell had left the FBI a year after the case ended and had just been made a full partner at the law firm of Hennessy, Fairbanks, and Hodges, one of the more prestigious firms in the District of Columbia.

It took seven phone calls over three days before he finally got through to her. "Ms. Farrell, I am Howard Jensen. You may not remember me from some five years ago but I was a D.C. homicide detective working on the Network case."

"Yes, Mr. Jensen, I do remember you. And, I also remember the sad event that unfolded for you. I still shake my head in total disbelief that such things can happen. What can I do for you?"

"I know you are very busy, and I do not want to unduly impose upon your time. Call it therapy, if you wish, but I am working on a book about the case and I am hoping writing about it will chase away some of the demons haunting my soul."

"And, where do I come in on all of this? I would rather not be mentioned by name in the book."

"And, so you won't. I would just like to discuss the interview you had with one of the ladies."

"I can help you with that. I have just been made partner here and time is a precious commodity. Even my private hours are filled, but I have discovered the only way to get anything done is to do two or three things at the same time. My son has a Little League baseball game at the last field in Dupont Park at 10:00 A.M. on Saturday. We can talk at the game if that works for you."

"Sure. Congrats on the partnership, and I really appreciate this."

"Fine. See you then."

Detectives take the unusual in stride, and Howard in particular had ceased to jump to conclusions on way out suggestions or plans. Meeting at a ball game would be a first, but if it led to something he would certainly keep it in mind for future meetings.

He was at the ball field at 9:45, and it was a beehive of activity. The players were warming up, and hordes of parents were milling around. He was not sure he would recognize Ms. Farrell, but she found him. She was not as young looking as he remembered, but she had a finely etched face, short hair neatly in place, and a slender body. A mystery even a detective cannot solve is how women get in to such tight jeans. He was not sure he had ever seen a lawyer in jeans before, but there was little he was sure about anymore. She led him away from the stands where most of the spectators were congregating to a more private place a bit away where she had unfolded two chairs.

As they sat, she pulled out a bottle of water from a cooler and offered it to him although she observed the cup of coffee he held. "Alright, Howard, let's get to it before I get carried away rooting for my son. Call me Vicky."

He felt he better be a bit social before jumping in with questions about the case. "Which one is your son?"

She pointed to a youngster near the pitching mound. "He may get to pitch a couple of innings later, depending how the scoring goes."

"Do you remember the Network lady you interviewed?"
"Sure. Grace Wharton."

Howard was a little taken aback as he expected to be stonewalled. "And do you know she survived the ordeal?"

"Yes. I am sure you know too that she is now a congresswoman, and one I admire. She has already done some commendable things bucking the partisan maneuvers. Proves one can surmount an adverse past. I had really not been with the FBI or the task force that long. With my law degree and strong computer skills, I was tapped for that interview. Grace was no ordinary woman. I could tell that even then. I had the feeling she was trapped by circumstance and I sensed she would break free at some point. It was also obvious that she knew nothing that would help with the investigation."

"Did you have a computer record of the interview?"

"Yes."

"What happened to it?"

"It got incorporated with all of the other interviews and then became part of the trial record."

Howard felt a knot in his stomach. He drained the last of the coffee from his cup as if that might help. "Oh, then the whole world potentially knew about her?"

"Not quite. Nobody told me I had to use real names, and I figured if I was in her place I wouldn't want my real name out there. So, I used Fay Wright. I wanted to give her a chance. Plus, I wasn't jeopardizing the case because she knew nothing and would not have been called as a witness."

"Wow! Vicky, you are quite a woman yourself!"

"The way I figure it, we have to look out for others in this mad world."

"I am glad you are on the good side."

"Howard, it is the only side."

"One more question and I'll leave you to enjoy this part of your life. Did any other FBI task force folk know about Grace?"

"Probably not, but I can't say for sure."

"Thanks a heap."

She extended her hand.   "Good luck."

He grasped the soft and well manicured hand, and knew it was another mark of a fine person when she did not recoil from his weathered calloused skin.   He was tempted to tell her about the blackmail scheme, but Vicky was one sharp woman and she must have figured that out on her own.

Howard walked from the ball field with a new admiration for some people in this world.   He just could not imagine Vicky as the blackmailer.   She knew Grace's background all along and could have used that information for her own gain long before this if such were her game.   He also knew who he would call if he ever needed a lawyer.

FIVE

Physically, Howard was at the gun shop, but his mind was trying to find a way to talk to the other three members of the FBI task force who were still at the Bureau without making three separate trips to their offices. A pesky customer kept distracting him before a welcome intrusion broke his train of thought completely. The perfume hit him before he saw her put the coffee cups and a brown bag he guessed had sandwiches in it on the counter. His initial thought was that he was glad he had showered and shaved this morning and his shirt was one he had only worn for two days.

Once in the back room munching on a ham sandwich and sipping the coffee, Grace showed him the note she received at her home in the mail. The handwritten letters were large and separated on a plain sheet of white paper, the writing purposely imitating the hand of a child and slanted in varying degrees to one side or the other.

**WITHDRAW NOW OR PAY THE PIPER.
NO ONE CAN HELP YOU.**

Howard handed the note back to her and took another sip of coffee before he spoke. "It is relatively easy to find your home address, so that doesn't add much to the mix."

She frowned, the voice hypnotic to a man with an empty life. "How serious do you think it is?"

"Still hard to tell. I think he or she will ask for money as well, in fact that might be really what they're after. The political part might be window dressing or setting the stage for the money angle. Even if the withdrawal is one of the wants, whether an amateur or a pro, they'll figure they might as well get some money out of this. Psychologically, it would add further seriousness to the request. So, anticipate that."

"Are you making any progress?"

"Some. Vicky Farrell who interviewed you when she was with the FBI may turn out to be one of your best friends. She is now a partner in a big D.C. law firm. She knows all about you and knowingly protected your identity back then by using a pseudonym. She figured you knew nothing so why get you involved in that mess. She is not our bird, I'm sure."

"I trust your evaluation, but all of this makes me highly suspicious."

Howard licked his cracked lips. That sandwich was good to a man without an appetite. "That's not a bad thing."

"It is if it distracts me from what I want and need to do."

"That is what the blackmailer is hoping for. Don't let it happen."

"I'll try."

Howard decided to telephone interview the FBI team, and if any loose threads were left hanging he would then try to arrange a personal meeting. It was evident from the calls they knew nothing and remembered little. They were crossed off the list.

Next was Rochelle Peters, the federal prosecuting attorney of both the Network officials and then the AWOLL women. She was still a prosecutor, and it took some doing to finally hook up with her. Another one of those successful and very busy women, and she agreed to talk to him only after he offered to buy her lunch.

At least she did not suggest a fancy French restaurant, but

even in a typical business eating establishment he was out of place in his wrinkled pants and faded shirt. He was beyond caring about that, and to her credit she did not seem to mind it at all. She had risen from the slums of Baltimore and was one of the first federal black attorneys to rise through the ranks on her own efforts and ability. The only word she tolerated was success.

"Alright, Mr. Jensen," she announced as she took up a large fork full of the side salad, "What sordid information do you think I can give you to spice up a book already steaming with its own spice?"

Howard took a sip of his coffee, ignoring the hamburger on his plate. "You were closely involved with the evil ones after I chased them down. What do you remember of the killers?"

"A tough bunch, for sure. People who make their own morality believe God is on their side. I wonder if God is with them as they rot in their cells."

"Did they know much about each of the victims?"

She finished the small salad and started on the bowl of beef stew. "Not as I remember. It was a cause and not a personal matter, so once the identity led to an address or other location to hunt them down, their viciousness took over."

Howard ordered another coffee, finally taking a bite from the thick hamburger. "Do you remember any of the names of the victims?"

"Not after all this time. Names got washed away in the blood. Justice was served, and that is the name of the game."

"How about those that luckily never became victims?"

"Immaterial, as I recall."

"What was the highlight of the trial?"

"Don't you mean the low light? Basically, it was an easy case to prove for me. The evidence was overwhelming. The jury deliberated for less than two hours, as I recall. The defense was only trying to avoid the death penalty, and in that they did succeed."

"And the trial against Mr. and Mrs. Blake?"

She took a long drink from her iced tea. "That was a different kettle of fish." A bite from the dinner roll and a spoon full of stew, "They were real clever in the scheme. He ran the network from several secret locations around the country. For awhile, it was thought there had to be others in running it, but he did it by himself. She did the recruiting of the ladies. They made a fortune, most of it forfeited and retrieved through diplomatic means from the offshore banks in exchange for not revealing names, account numbers, and the like, or pointing to others who might have been involved. Anyway, he is serving twenty years in Lewinsville Federal Penitentiary, and she still has three years to go at Mankinville Prison for Women."

He took another bite of the hamburger, now cold but he hardly noticed it. "Did the names of any of the Network ladies come up at the trial?"

She paused in the eating process for a moment. "Not that I remember. I didn't need names to prove what they did, how they did it, and how much they made. Even the names of the foreign nations that paid dearly for what staggers my imagination was inconsequential." Another pause, and her voice accentuated an afterthought. "If you mention me by name in the book you will need my written permission."

"You mean you won't put that on the back of the receipt for me buying you your lunch?"

She chuckled. "I can't really accept you paying for my lunch. You should know that. I'm a public official and barred by strict ethics from receiving any kind of favors. I only enticed you to that point to test how earnest you were about picking my brain. We're Americans, but we are going Dutch."

It was his turn to smile, even though there would always be some residual pain in doing that. Rochelle Peters was more help than he dared to hope for. A trip to Mankinville seemed to be in the cards. "At least, let me leave the tip."

"You may do that. I also have a tip for you. Writing a book is not a good excuse for getting information."

Another astute woman one step ahead of him, and another lesson for him to learn. Forthright is better than forthwrong if there was such a word. Or, in the final analysis is it all just forthcoming? Even though black, there was no way she was a blackmailer.

SIX

All prisons are drab, and Mankinville Prison for Women was as drab as it gets. More than a thousand women crammed between dingy walls and seemingly carrying signs reading menaces to themselves and society. Howard, in his early days, thought there must be a better way than a prison system, but he could not ever think of one and then just accepted what was there without thinking about it.

Howard was a little surprised that Pauline Blake had agreed to see him, but he was not going to psychoanalyze her. At this point, she seemed like the most likely suspect and he wanted to push that.

Even in prison garb, there was little doubt that Pauline was a classy woman. She was eloquent in both mannerisms and speech, and if dressed to the hilt no man or woman could probably deny her overtures. She could even be a recruiter for the Marines. Howard guessed she had convinced many a woman she could get rich on her back in bed. Pauline confirmed that in one of her initial observations as she sat across from him behind the table in the visiting room. "A woman's most valuable asset is her body. Nobody is interested in her mind."

Howard made a note in his own mind not to tell that to Vicky or Rochelle. "Is it alright if I take notes?"

"As long as you promise not to use my real name in the book. Soon, I will be out of here and I intend to make a new life."

"Sure."

"What do you want to know?"

"Explain the recruiting process to me?"

"Do you want the long version or the short one?"

"Whichever."

Dark brown eyes riveted on the coffee stain on his shirt. "Parties, professional parties, proved to be the most productive place to meet women frustrated with lack of advancement in a male world. I would zero in on ones there by themselves, and I just knew they would be ripe for suggestions on means to bypass the system for easy and quick riches. An unattached woman was like a fish out of water, and I didn't even have to reel them in. The promise of a luxurious life style, clothes, travel, and expensive jewelry, and all the trimmings, is hard to turn away from. It was never a hard sell, and often victory was a foregone conclusion. Most of them turned out to be really good and, of course, everything I promised came to pass. They were happy and I was happy. It would still be a total panacea if those nut cases did not butt in."

"Did you keep any records or other kinds of notes?"

"No. That clearly came out at the trial. Our success and, supposedly, our security blanket, was not having any written or computer records. Even as to the accounting end, any records were destroyed as soon as we were notified that foreign payments had been received and the ladies were paid."

"Do you remember any of the women?"

Smug has its own distinctive look. "I remember them all."

"And, if one of them got murdered, what was your reaction?"

"I was baffled as you were."

"Was there any reason or cause to silence any of them?"

"We kept them in the dark. They knew only what we allowed them to know."

"Do you have any contact with the ones that are still alive?"

She rubbed her arm as if there was a pain that would not go

away. "There is no reason at my end or theirs."

"I hope to interview them and find out if they are now living different lives. Do you know where I can contact any of them?"

"There has been no way I can keep track of them. I would like to know what you find out. I suppose I will have to read the book." She rubbed her arm again. "Easy money is hard to turn from. My guess would be that once a whore always a whore."

Again, her use of words registered in his mind. "You had easy money."

"Yes, but I am not a whore."

"There can be no exceptions to such a fate?"

"I suppose if a lucky break comes along."

"Like what?"

"Finding a rich husband, or turning to religion, or getting old and sick, or being imprisoned. Prison can change anyone's outlook."

"What about doing public service?"

Her hesitation was telling. "Hollywood, maybe. Public service is a waste of a woman's talents."

"So, I gather you would not consider anything like that for yourself or anything that might wind you back in prison?"

The smug look surfaced again. "That's for sure."

"Not even for an easy buck?"

"No buck is easy if it means coming back to this place."

She did not sound convincing, and he did not believe her anyway. Call it a detective's instinct. Maybe it was the way she looked so smug. Or, maybe it was the way she rubbed her arm. But, if there really were no records, and a thorough search had been made for them, how did Pauline expect to pull this off if challenged? Of course, it was not an absolute that there were no records. They could have been very well hidden or camouflaged. How did she hope to prevail against a now powerful and influential woman? If she was the blackmailer, why the political front without going for money right away? Doing blackmail from prison would be hard enough if straight forward. Why make it more difficult with a political subterfuge? Howard still believed that money was the true goal here. If he was wrong about that, Pauline would no longer be a suspect.

SEVEN

Howard discussed with Len the possibility that Pauline Blake was the blackmailer. All of the pieces were there, but they did not fall neatly into place. It would be especially difficult to do all of this from prison. If she were the one, a person or persons on the outside was probably in on it. That raised its own complexities and uncertainties.

Len had found out as much as he could about the Blakes. There was not much as they tried primarily to be obscure to pull off their schemes. The one promising lead was that they had an adult son living in San Francisco. He had been thoroughly investigated and questioned extensively by the FBI. His denial of any knowledge or participation in anything that went on was accepted in the absence of any proof to the contrary. Search warrants had been issued and nothing was found in his home or business that might incriminate him. If there had been any records, and if he ever had or still had any or all of them, such had been successfully hidden. However, blood is thicker than water and it was certainly plausible that the younger Blake may not be as innocent as professed. Before attempting to speak with him, Howard wanted to make a trip to Lewinsville to question the elder Mr. Blake.

Grace telephoned, telling him that he had predicted the next step correctly. A note, similar in style, came to her office. She read it to him.

YOU CAN STAY IN OFFICE
FOR $100,000 IN CASH –
INSTRUCTIONS TO COME

He had her read it again just so he could let his damaged soul linger in that silken voice a bit longer. For an instant it was a calming effect. Then his thoughts would turn to his beautiful Alice and his heart would cry.

After reading it to him, Grace continued quickly, "I don't have that much money, but I could borrow it. I would only pay it if they surrendered whatever proof they have."

Howard almost felt like a parent talking to a naive child. "Not feasible, Grace, on all fronts. First, paying only assures further requests for money later. They will know they have you in the bag. Second, there is no guarantee if what they do have is the only proof or is the only copy if it is just one thing."

It was a tone of exasperation. "Then, what do I do?"

"It is not easy, but nothing. You'll force their hand by doing nothing. Hopefully, they'll contact you by telephone or in person, and you will be prepared to concentrate on every detail of the voice, words, inflection, and if in person appearance and gestures. I think by telephone is the safe bet, but you have to be prepared for anything."

He filled her in on his impression about Pauline Blake. "I may be close or still way out in left field. Just remember the one truism, you never get rid of a blackmailer by paying blackmail. I have to also caution you that they may get frustrated or angry and try to show you they mean business. So, some show of force might be tried."

The sultry voice cracked ever so slightly. "Like what?"

"It could be anything. Probably an act of vandalism like a slashed tire or a broken window. You need to be strong and, hopefully, in all of this they'll make a mistake."

"I have a burglar alarm at the house and the Capitol Police at the office."

"That's good. I doubt they will do anything physically to you. They want your money, not you."

"That is not comforting."

"Not meant to be."

"Get me out of this, Howard, please."

"I'm working on it."

Howard had been surprised that Pauline Blake had agreed to see him. He was further surprised when Homer Blake consented to a prison visit. After all, he still had fifteen years to serve behind bars and being in a book was not going to be of any help. Perhaps, Pauline had told him about the visit and she asked him to verify and downplay whatever she might have said. Anything and everything was possible. That kind of premise leaves all of the doors and windows open.

Compared to his classy wife, Homer Blake was rather nondescript. Obviously older and shorter than his wife, they made a strange couple. A bushy mustache did not compensate for sunken eyes. His voice was weak and accentuated the monotone transmission. "Well, Mr. Jensen, let's get this over with."

"I won't keep you long. Do you get any visitors?"

He shuffled his feet and twirled his thumbs nervously. "You're the first in over three years."

"I suppose the Network did not lead to popularity?"

"It wasn't supposed to."

"What was it to lead to?"

"A fortune."

"And, it did, didn't it?"

"Yeah, but never got to spend much of it or enjoy it."

"Breaking the law does that."

"I don't need a lecture."

"Everyone needs a lecture about the difference between right and wrong every once and awhile."

"Consider it done." His impatience was obvious. "What specifically do you want from me?"

"Do you know the whereabouts of any of the women who are still alive?"

"Why would you think I would know that now?"

"I am asking the questions."

"The answer is emphatically a no."

"Did you have any personal interaction with them early on?"

"Do you mean sex?"

"That, or just a friendship."

"Never got close to any of them, and did not ever see most of them in person. Any communications were just addressed to the whats and whens."

"What about the whys?"

"None ever asked, and I never volunteered anything."

"Do you talk to your wife?"

"We are allowed a call a week."

"What do you talk about?"

"The future."

"No talk of the past?"

"What for?"

"When you agreed to see me, did you have something in mind that you wanted to talk about?"

"Just not to portray us in the book as monsters. We just filled a void that someone else would have done if we didn't do it. It was all business, plain and simple."

"You could have told me that on the phone."

"Also, leave my wife out of this completely."

"No names, I promise, but facts are facts."

"Interview over." He rose from the two-way window and

motioned for the guard to take him away.

Howard sensed there was more going on than the Blakes were willing to talk about. It made it more imperative to talk to their son.

❖

EIGHT

It could be said that Harmon Blake had it all. With wealthy parents, he went to all of the finest schools. He was denied nothing. A desire to travel all over the world was fulfilled, and he turned that compulsion and experience by establishing his own fancy and highly successful travel agency in San Francisco. A palatial home, beautiful wife, smart children, produced a picture perfect man. The fallacy in it all was that his parents were crooks. Was he one as well?

Howard was prepared to go to California if necessary. A telephone conversation with Harmon was inconclusive, and he sensed that because of Harmon's extremely guarded statements that his parents had alerted him as to Howard's interest. Were they savvy enough to know that the book writing was a ruse?

When Howard suggested a personal meeting after concocting a story that he had to be in San Francisco for an additional reason, Harmon agreed to see him but also made it clear that he did not really have anything to add to the topics discussed on the telephone. Howard knew he needed the personal interview to fully assess the probability of Harmon's culpability. If he had not agreed to see him, the suspicion would be there for sure if he was part of any blackmail scheme. Howard knew that was a lot of ifs.

Howard had never been to San Francisco. In fact, he had never been west of Chicago. As a D.C. homicide detective for all of those years, jurisdiction was confined to the District so there was no need to travel for his work. He also had little funds for personal travel and did not have the desire to see different places. Yet, San Francisco was a charming city, and the hills and cable cars were a sight for old tired eyes. It would have been a nice place to visit with Alice. It always came back to that. Any life he could have had began and ended with her. The killer knew too well that he had been killed as well, a strange kind of death where a particular suffering does not end.

World Dreams Travel had its own striking building smack in the downtown area. When Howard entered the main office, there were many things to impress a visitor, especially a shell of a man. The walls were lined with large and colorful poster images of exotic places around the world. A half dozen desks arranged in a u-shape were occupied by young and beautiful women. Howard guessed that Harmon had a sexual appetite outside of his marriage or, at least, he needed to have temptation close at hand. A special beauty occupied a desk as his personal secretary just outside of his office to the rear. Howard was fairly certain that Harmon must have recruited ladies for the Network. It was much too easy to do.

Harmon made Howard wait for twenty minutes before he was led in to the office by the beauty. Howard surmised that Harmon was making a subtle statement that when the interview started he would be in control of it.

As he would have guessed, Harmon was handsome and impeccably dressed in a black suit that must have been custom-made because the fit was so perfect. There was not a wrinkle in the fabric, a far cry from the old pants and sports jacket Howard was wearing. Harmon's abstract tie probably cost as much as Howard was paying for the hotel he was staying at. A sociologist would have a field day defining the contrast between the two men.

They shook hands without Harmon getting up from his seat behind the ornate desk. He motioned for Howard to sit in the chair before the desk. "Can I get you a drink." The voice was slightly high-pitched but refined.   High class and high brow meets the gutter man.

"Coffee, black, would be appreciated."

Harmon buzzed the secretary, and within a minute she brought in a fancy mug of coffee.   Wearing a form-fitting short red dress, the secretary was truly gorgeous and Howard could not help but stare at her coming and going.   He could not take his eyes off of her, and he guessed that Harmon was watching as well.

Howard took a sip of the coffee.   It was hot and fresher than what he was used to, and it was easy to conclude that riches bring with it a whole bunch of privileges and conveniences.   It was another world to a man who never did have anything and never would. "Thanks for the coffee."

"It's a special blend I get from Columbia."

"Business must be good."

"It has been better.   Terrorism has put a damper on things. The traveling class is reluctant to go as much as they used to."

"The world will never be the same, that is for sure."   Howard wondered if Harmon picked up on the inference.

If he did, he ignored it.   "Well, Mr. Jensen, I am very busy so let's proceed with whatever you think I can add to our prior conversation."

"As I told you, and they probably told you, I talked to your parents.   Prison can have two effects on people.   It either loosens or tightens the tongue.   They both gave me a heap of generalities but few specifics on their activities.   Generalities will not fly in a book."

Harmon picked up a pen from the desk top and rolled it between his fingers.   Howard liked to think it was a nervous reaction. "I was not part of anything so not privy to what, where, or why anything was going on.   The police cleared me of any involvement. Whatever they told you is far more than I know."

"Will your mother come here when she gets out?"

"She knows she is welcome here, but I don't think she has decided on anything yet." After a pause, he added, "I do not talk to her often and when we do she is more interested in what I am doing and what the grandchildren are up to than in confiding her thoughts to me."

Howard thought that was a strange statement, or maybe he just wanted to read some strangeness into it. "There was a Network group of ladies right here in San Francisco, I believe. None of them were murdered."

He looked away for an instant before looking at Howard. "Yeah. Right under my nose and I didn't have a clue."

"If the ladies traveled to a convention in another city, did you make arrangements for them?"

"Possibly. If I did, I wouldn't have known their business or motives for travel. My staff would probably have handled it. I sign off on the final documents but it is mere procedure. As long as we get paid there is little to be gained by being nosy."

"Did you ever know any of the Network ladies?"

"If I did, I wouldn't have known about their involvement."

"Do you know any of them now?"

"No, and don't care to. Any hint of scandal would be bad for business."

Howard thought that was a strange thing to say. It was similar to Grace's pronouncement about politics. "One more question and I'll let you be, although I could use another coffee. He would have liked the coffee as he usually does, especially one of such quality, but he also wanted to see the secretary in action again. He waited until he had the coffee in hand. "I have been able to talk to a few of the Network ladies that I have been able to find. They have all gone on to other pursuits, so to speak. Yet, they all have one thought in common. That is, their days in the Network are not completely history."

Harmon interrupted him with a slight agitation. "What do they mean by that?"

Howard drained the last of the coffee from the mug and placed it on the desk. "Mighty good coffee. Thanks." He rose and before he turned to leave he muttered, "They all have the feeling they are being watched."

As the plane landed in Washington, Howard wondered if the seed he planted would result in anything. As he told Len and Grace, all was not Kosher in San Francisco, but it was more of a feeling than a fact. Yet, in the world of crime, a feeling can easily ripen into a fact.

❖

NINE

Len was able to find out information from his original notes about the location of a former Network lady who had, as did Grace, gone down a different path. His reasoning followed the line of greed. If the blackmailer was after money, and if he or she or they had a full or partial list of the identities of the original Network participants, then it would seem highly likely that if a former lady had risen to some level of prominence, she would already have been or soon would be a blackmail victim. The Network secret brought with it a particular vulnerability.

It was going on two years that Norma Whitestone had a leading role in a highly successful off Broadway play. Full audiences and a long advance ticket sale spurred by early rave reviews promised a long run for the show. Her home address and telephone number were unavailable, and the calls Howard made to her at the theater were not returned. It looked like he would have to take a trip to New York City.

He telephoned Grace about Norma and the proposed trip. Just to listen to that captivating voice was incentive enough to make the call. It dawned on him that it was not just Grace's voice but there was a deeper connection. Alice's voice was so cultured and resonated to spellbind him as well. It was if he was listening to Alice each time Grace spoke. Little wonder he was just a ghost of his past. There were too many haunting memories engulfing him.

Grace was quick to admit that there was little comfort that

others were being blackmailed. She had also not heard anything further from the blackmailer and wondered what that might mean. Howard indicated that a worry and wait ploy is often used by a blackmailer, but there was little chance that there had been a change of heart.

He took the train to New York. A good story, far afield from the true objective, would have to be concocted to talk to Norma alone. After all, if she was being blackmailed, he could be taken for the blackmailer. If she was not a victim, with her now famous stance and Howard's presumption that she was beautiful as validated by her picture on the billboard in front of the theater, she was probably approached by a vast assortment of men for a variety of reasons. Then there was the reality of why in the world would anyone want to talk to the likes of him?

Settled in at a hotel near the theater, he decided that honesty was the best tact. He wrote a note to her.

Dear Ms. Whitestone:

My name is Howard Jensen. I am a retired D.C. homicide detective. I am working on a blackmail case, in confidence, for a former acquaintance. If you could spare me a few minutes, I am hoping you can assist me in this investigation. It would be much appreciated.

> *Howard Jensen*
> *Cosmopolitan Hotel*
> *533 Broadway*
> *629-4400, Rm. 612*

He put the note in an envelope, sealed it, and addressed it to her at the theater and marked it as confidential. If he could not approach her personally, he would ask that the envelope be delivered to her.

He was not allowed back stage, but gave the stage doorman a twenty dollar bill to give the envelope to her. After the performance, he waited at the back door. He was hoping to see her, but after two hours he either had missed her or she had exited a different way. Disappointment and weariness led him back to the hotel. He ordered a coffee and a ham sandwich from room service and then fell asleep without undressing. His clothes looked like he slept in them anyway, and this time he did.

The telephone jarred him awake. Sun was streaming through the window, and he glanced at the clock on the bedside table. It was twenty after nine. "Hello," was painful to muster.

"Mr. Jensen. This is Norma Whitestone. I did get your note, but I already know all about you."

He should have figured that one out but blundered ahead anyway, "How is that?"

"Not only did I see the documentary, but I have a special interest and connection to your past."

He was not much of a detective if he did not see that coming. "Then, will you kindly see me?"

"There is a bench right along Central Park at 63rd Street and Fifth Avenue. There is usually a hot dog stand nearby. I will meet you there at 11:00 o'clock if you can make it."

His voice was clearer than his eyes. "Sure."

She hung up without saying good-bye. "This is going to be challenging," he said to himself. Ball fields and park benches were now his meeting places. He ordered three coffees from room service and saved the third one for after his shower. He put on a fresh set of wrinkled clothing and headed out.

It was easy to find the park bench. She was not there yet, so he got a hot dog and coffee from the stand and sat on the bench. A steady stream of people came by and they were not interested in him and would not dare to sit by a bum.

She did not look like her picture, but was extremely attractive and well dressed. He knew it was her when she hesitated before sitting down. A variation of a princess and a pauper came to mind. "Mr. Jensen, I had to make sure I was not followed."

That already answered many of his questions. "I know it is not comforting to know you are not the only one being blackmailed, but it does help from my end."

Long eyelashes over piercing brown eyes blinked nervously. He had not seen eyelashes that long before and wondered if they were real. Was anything real anymore? "How is that?"

"It is either someone who played a major role in the past or has documentation extensive enough to cover at least two cities."

"This is the last thing I need in my life." A large tear formed at the corner of a brown eye.

"I can understand that. When and how did it start?"

"Nine days ago. I got a note at the theater, in the same way yours was delivered. This is it."

He unfolded the paper. It was the same child-like scrawl and a similar threat. It told her to quit the play or the whole world would know she was a whore. "Have you shown this to anyone or told anyone about it?"

"No. I didn't see any point to it. Besides then I would have to give an explanation, or a confession, depending on how you want to look at it. Why now I keep asking myself."

"I have made some progress narrowing this down. But, it is solely based on the expectation that you now have enough money to pay them off. They really don't want to ruin your career. They're after money. You will undoubtedly get a follow-up note indicating you can keep on acting if you will pay up."

"I am just starting to get comfortable financially. The money

I had as well as everything else was all forfeited, but you know that. I can't raise any substantial amount. Could they be after something else? There is too much history here. Should I fear for my life?"

"I think this is purely greed driven. Yet, take every precaution that you can. Try not to let it sway you from what you are doing. Any change in your demeanor will assure them they have you where they want you. Your success has made you vulnerable, but you don't want them to know that. How close were you to people in the Network?"

"What do you mean?"

"Did you know who recruited you? Did you ever meet or know anything about those who ran the operation?"

"Foolishly, and I was desperate at the time to escape a hapless life, I answered an ad for an escort. Nobody interviewed me in person, all I got was a phone call and was asked some basic questions. Then, I was given a trial run at a local convention and was given written instructions that I received by a courier with orders to destroy them after I read them. It was the same after that. I never met or talked to anyone. I guess I was lulled to submission with what was easy money. I briefly chatted with other ladies at parties but I do not remember anything that would relate to this. I suppose I should have been more alert to things, and I know now I should not have started in that. Once the murders started, I was scared stiff. Sorry, I'm not much help."

He felt a pang of sympathy for her, and if he could have expressed his feelings he would have. He might even have hugged her, but his personal barrier prevented him from being the human being he would like to be. "You could not anticipate all that unfolded. Nobody could. We need to communicate with each other. Is there a way to do that?"

She pulled out a scrap of paper from her handbag. "This is a private telephone number."

He wrote down his cell phone number on a paper he tore out of his notebook. He closed the book without taking a single note during the interview. "This will work out. Believe that."

In a whisper he barely heard, she replied, "I'll try." She stood up and within seconds was lost in the lunch time crowd walking along the sidewalk.

He finished eating the hot dog, and as he took the last swig of the coffee, he muttered to the air, "Now what?"

TEN

Even if he was a super duper fortune teller or had unusual psychic powers, Howard would not have guessed at what was about to happen. If there was an apple cart, it was not only overturned it was completely destroyed.

A telephone call came for him at the gun shop. "Hello, Howard, this is Rochelle Peters." Before he could even shout out how come she knew he worked at the gun shop, she exclaimed, "I thought you would want to know that there has been an event of interest. Harmon Blake was found murdered in San Francisco." How he held on to the receiver he will never know, but he was speechless. She continued, "I presume your silence is the same shock I felt hearing the news. Details are sketchy, but this is what I know. He was found in the morning in his office shot twice. There was apparently a scuffle and nothing was missing. So far, the San Francisco authorities have no leads." She stopped for a minute in case he wanted to say something, but she pictured an ashen face and a tongue tied in a knot. "The only reason they notified me was because of the legal history of my connection with the Blakes. They asked me if I knew if he had any enemies, but I don't know much about him since my major focus in all of this was his parents. I didn't mention you, but they did. They asked me if I knew you. They know you were a recent visitor."

Len added some sense of order when Howard told him about the turn of events. "After all", he opined, "it may have been a totally unrelated act. From what you observed, he was surrounded by enticing sex objects. We have seen time and time again that jealousy or other emotions can enter the picture and lead to murder. It does throw a monkey wrench into the mix, but it certainly does not mean you are on the wrong track. Give Mrs. Blake a few days to absorb the news and then confront her. It might be revealing."

It was difficult to conjure up a picture of the beauty blasting Harmon away but it could have happened that way. Of course, if there had been a true struggle it stretched the imagination to believe that any of the office vixens could not be overpowered unless two or more were involved. The upsetting scenario would be if the murder was related to the blackmail. That would mean that others were involved and dissension in the ranks spelled trouble all the way around.

The San Francisco police did contact him by way of the D.C. Homicide Bureau, and probably because of his law enforcement connections they bought his story about seeing Harmon for purposes of the book. Howard felt bad about withholding vital information and disguising his real reason for the visit, but he figured it would be best to let the investigation take its course and if later it came down that they should know about the blackmail scheme he would open up.

Without calling ahead, Howard went to Mankinville figuring an unannounced visit might throw Pauline further off guard. She could refuse to see him, but he counted on the fact that she probably needed someone to talk to about her son. That part he got right. What he did not predict was how emotionally distraught she was. He could barely make out her words through the sobbing. Puffy eyes indicated an extended period of weeping. "They won't even let me go to his funeral," she lamented.

His tone was truly sympathetic. "You should contact your lawyer."

"I have, but I haven't heard back from him."

"They should let you go."

Her sobbing increased and her entire body was shaking. "They should do a lot of things."

If he ever had any scruples, he probably would think twice about taking advantage of her weak emotional state. A detective with scruples is not much of a detective. "Was he helping you with getting the money?"

The sobs abated before she spoke in a hoarse whisper, "You knew it all, didn't you?"

"I had my suspicions."

She dabbed her eyes with a tissue. "I guess I am not as clever as I thought I was." A loud sigh was followed by a guttural string of profanity, well out-of-place from one who was once high society. "Now the only thing I get is what I lost, the only thing that truly matters."

"You still have your daughter-in-law and the grandchildren."

"That bitch is probably happy to see him go." She bent her head down to her knees. "It's all not the same without him."

He was tempted to probe the wife angle, but the murder was not his case. "The authorities will want to know from you if you know anything, particularly if he had any enemies."

She bolted erect. "They already questioned me."

"Did you tell them about your involvement?"

A form of tortured laughter came out. "Do you think I am crazy?"

"What are you going to do about that now?"

She snickered. "It's over."

"Are you sure about that?"

"What are you insinuating?"

"I believe someone else on the outside is involved in this."

Her response was a bit too quick and a bit too loud.

"There isn't."

"What if it doesn't stop?"

The old smugness raised its ugly head. "It has dead stopped!"

"If it has, my silence is golden. If not, you'll be very old and decrepit by the time you get out of here."

She snapped at him, "You can't threaten me!"

"It's not a threat. It's a dose of reality."

"Some forms of reality can be overwhelming."

"Now, who is threatening?"

"Take it as you wish."

"Is Homer involved in this?"

A moment of silence and her voice softened. Tears, perhaps of a different kind, rolled down from her eyes. "Please leave him out of this."

"I will if you have been completely honest with me."

"I have been."

Howard was not completely convinced. He hoped he was wrong. "We'll see."

When he telephoned Grace and Norma, he hedged his report of the events. The blackmail might be over, but only time would support that. His detective's instinct told him this was all too easy a way for it to end. Figuring out who killed Harmon might bring the true answer.

ELEVEN

It took less than a month for the San Francisco police to arrest Harmon's wife on a murder charge. Apparently, she had caught him cheating on her more than once. As happens, especially for a woman who reportedly had a history of a violent temper, rage led to the worst of solutions.

Two months passed, and by all indications it appeared that the blackmail scheme that was there was now no more. Grace gave him a substantial monetary bonus, but he knew that no amount of money was going to relieve him from the anguish he was now free to sink into even more now that the investigatory involvement was over. Any ember of light and warmth in his soul was already gone, and he returned to a day-to-day bare existence. He did not even have the sultry voice now to edge him on. He drank lots of coffee more as a habit than as a form of enjoyment, and he further distanced himself from people and events. He even declined an invitation from Len for a visit. Added torment came from seeing any woman on the street or elsewhere who resembled Alice. He did not even have enough memories of her to grab hold of to prevent sinking even lower.

He had a surprise visitor at the gun shop. Rochelle Peters must have taken a liking to him or felt so sorry for him that she had to see for herself that he was still in the vertical. Of course, a four-day stubble and soiled clothes must have steeped the outlook to pity.

When he looked up he saw her staring at him. "A sight not for sightseers," she offered in a soft voice.

"For sure," was the extent of his response.

"I was in the neighborhood, so I thought I would drop in to see how my favorite lunch companion is doing. Felice Blake has been indicted for Harmon Blake's murder and, sadly, two beautiful children are now in foster care and will spend a lifetime trying to avoid a connection to a whole family of criminals. I have been in this business too long to deny that life can be quite cruel. I also see what it has done to you. Can I help you in any way?"

He cleared a dry throat. "Kind words from a kind lady. I need nothing and want nothing, but I will put you on Santa's nice list."

She smiled. "I'll tell you a secret nobody else knows. Santa is a black man. You are the only white guy on his nice list."

He forced a half smile. He could love this woman if he could ever love again, just as he could love Vicky. He could count the good folks on the fingers of one hand. Such people would always be special in what remained of his life. "You're a sweetie."

"So are you." She patted his dangling arm and was out the door.

The coffee he reached for behind him on the back counter was cold but he did not notice. He just stared at the door waiting for Alice to come in next.

TWELVE

A few days later Howard's cell phone rang. It had been a long time since he had a call on it. He could not even remember when he had last charged it. It was the sultry voice but the tone was anything but pleasant. "I just got another note! Good grief! What is going on?"

His head was far from clear, but he knew this was not what he wanted to hear. It made no sense. The only theory that popped up in his clouded mind was that Pauline could not resist what she felt was an easy mark and had recruited a new messenger. Why she would risk further time in the slammer was beyond him at the moment. "Keep your cool, Grace. Read me the note."

Her tone had leveled and she spoke methodically. "Time is not on your side. This will be your last chance. Raise $100,000 in small bills, unmarked, and you will be told when and where to deliver it. Tell no one or all will know and despise you."

One conclusion jumped out at him. "We're dealing with someone else now. The use of the word 'despise' tells me that the new blackmailer is more educated."

"I'll leave you to figure that out. What do I do?"

"As before, do nothing." Howard took a deep breath and tried to get his faculties in working condition. He hoped Alice would wait until he was finished here. "I'm back on it."

He telephoned Norma. She had not received a note, and Howard told her to expect it and to call him when she did. She was very upset, believing this was over and done with. She was also instructed to do nothing.

Howard called Len and he was equally surprised. They discussed the possibilities. They both thought Pauline was out of it and they were dealing with someone new. She could have tipped someone else off. Someone in the investigation of Harmon's murder might have come across information that triggered this action. Or, Harmon might have had an accomplice all along. Anyway, it was almost like starting over again, and Howard was not quite sure he was up to it. Len attempted to bolster him and offered to help in any way he could.

A quick visit was made to Pauline Blake. She swore she had completely let this go and had told nobody about it. Howard believed her. He even believed that Homer did not know anything about it at all. It could not be someone new that had come out of the woodwork because the latest note was built upon the earlier ones. So, this left some aspect of Harmon's former life that created the opportunity. Could he have gotten close enough to the beauty or one of the other temptresses to have told one of them about the scheme or to have involved them in the ploy? Could one of them have found something about it in Harmon's papers before the police went through them? Was there an outside person who had been helping him? If so, why the time delay? Len offered to go to San Francisco, but Howard knew he had to do it since he already knew the situation there and had made contact with the employees.

It was early afternoon when he arrived at Harmon's travel agency. The door was locked and a large closed sign was hung on the door with a notation that they were sorry for the inconvenience. Howard peered through the glass and noticed a figure moving around. He knocked forcefully. A woman that he recognized as one of the office workers unlocked the door and let him in. She was petite, young, and beautiful. She was wearing jeans and a simple blouse, but there was no denying her allure. "Mr. Jensen. You are back and I am sure you know what has happened. What can I do for you?"

"I had not quite finished my business with Mr. Blake. Maybe, you can help me tie up the ends."

"I doubt it. I am the office manager and here trying to see through the clients arrangements that had already been made and paid for. Those monies will go to the estate and the children will get it when they are older. Unfortunately, that may be all that there is. The building and business are up for sale, but Mr. Blake owed a bunch of money on both, as well as on his house. Business has not been good the last couple of years and he borrowed whatever he could."

That would answer the mystery of why the blackmail scheme developed so late. The need did not arise until business went south. Perhaps, there were loan sharks involved adding pressure for payments. Howard believed Harmon was too astute to have revealed the blackmail scheme to loan sharks unless his life was threatened, and even then he would not have given names because that was his life insurance. The wife messed it all up. "Did Mr. Blake have a romantic involvement with anyone here at the office?"

"The police asked me the same question. He is dead. It's best all things be laid to rest."

"But, it might be important for other matters."

"Such as what?"

"Other people he may have owed money or favors to."

"Only his personal secretary, Darby Hollister, would know that."

"Do you know where I might contact her?"

"She moved back home soon after the murder and when the police finished questioning her."

"Where is that?"

"Washington, D.C."

Howard nearly keeled over backwards. "Do you have an address?"

"No, but she mentioned once that her father is a judge back there."

"Thanks. You have been a big help."

Len researched Simon Hollister, a senior judge on the D.C. Circuit Court for thirty-seven years. He had an impeccable reputation and was highly commended for trial oversight and extensive written judicial opinions. He was married to a high society woman for forty years and had two sons besides the daughter, Darby. He lived in a house off Rock Creek Parkway, interestingly a few houses away from where one of the Network ladies had been eliminated.

Howard thought he better get an inside opinion before he tried to hook up with the daughter. He telephoned Vicky Farrell, and instead of waiting three days as he did the first time, he was put through to her right away. Howard's name was now most likely on some form of acceptable list, and if so probably the only acceptable list he had ever been on.

"What's up, Howard?"

"I just need a quick lawyer assessment of a judge."

The voice was sincerely consoling. "Are you in some kind of trouble?"

"No, not yet as far as I know. Just trying to tie up some loose ends. Do you know anything about Judge Simon Hollister?"

"I haven't had a case before him. The word here at the firm is to avoid his courtroom if possible. He is tough and comes down hard on attorneys, so it is told. Other than that, he is known as a straight arrow. Do you want me to ask around some more?"

"No, that is fine. I just thought there might be something there that is not in his bio." Howard felt the need to say something personal. "Is your son pitching these days?"

"Yes, and doing well. Thanks for asking."

"And you, thanks for not asking why I am interested in the judge."

"I have enough in my own bee's wax. Call me if you need to know anything else."

"I will. You are my hero."

"Glad to hear that. Bye."

Another confirmation that Vicky was one of the best. Her son was one lucky pitcher.

THIRTEEN

From what Howard and Len could piece together, Darby Hollister was a kind of black sheep in the family. To follow in her father's footsteps, as well as her two older brothers who became lawyers, she went to Yale Law School. Her father was an alumni and a benefactor so she had no trouble getting in. Staying in was the problem. Her grades were poor and she had been disciplined for poor attendance. The only law school that would accept her as a transfer student was Golden Gate University in San Francisco. She did not last six months there, but stayed in San Francisco doing modeling work when she could get it. Her father apparently gave her a hefty allowance and she put that and her good looks to advance up the social ladder. How she became Harmon's personal secretary was unknown, but through her budding social contacts she was probably able to get him some good clients. Len theorized that Harmon tried to recruit her for the Network, but she would have none of that because she did not need the money. Somehow, they figured he had gotten her to commit to being his mistress, and the personal secretary front was a way for them to be together. Howard wondered how much he would be able to get out of her even if he was able to talk to her.

There had been a bunch of surprises in what was left of his life, and it certainly was another one when Darby Hollister agreed to see him. He took a way out chance and just went to the house. Her mother answered the doorbell and he could almost see her nose wrinkle up when she saw an apparent panhandler standing there.

After he explained who he was and why he was there, she left him standing there with the door closed as she went back inside. A few minutes later Darby opened the door. She was in a short housecoat tied with a sash at the waist. Even in what would be termed a frumpy attire, she was still a perfect beauty with magnificent shapely legs set in furry slippers. Long flowing red hair framed a face with perfect features Her complexion was the clearest he had ever remembered seeing, and he could only guess that a wealthy upbringing has natural perks. "Come in, Mr. Jensen. I remember you from San Francisco and I have already told the maid to get you a coffee. Follow me to the library where we can talk in private."

He would have followed her anyway, but it was better she invited him. The library was a windowless room with shelves from floor to ceiling filled with law books. A rectangular table in the center of the room had six upholstered chairs around it. Recessed lights in the ceiling bathed the room with bright light. She pulled out two chairs to face one another and motioned for him to sit. After she sat she crossed the shapely legs and the housecoat raised nearly to the top of the full thighs. Her eyes followed his. "Even old men can appreciate what they see."

He was not much of a philosopher but the gem came out anyway. "It is easy to appreciate what you know you can never have."

The maid knocked and brought in two mugs of coffee. His eyes shifted to the steam rising from the coffee. That he could have.

"I know why you are here, Howard. May I call you Howard?"

"Howard it is, Darby. If you know why I am here and open with me, I can be gone before the third mug of coffee."

He thought that might bring a smile to the full lips, but she was stone-faced. "Here it is in a nutshell, Howard. You can ask questions later if you have any. My father is fond of saying that criminals usually slip up because they are stupid or desperate. Harmon was desperate. He knew why you came to San Francisco and that you were on to him. I'm getting ahead of myself. Let me back up. After I dropped out of law school, I decided to stay in San Francisco. I modeled and got swept up in the society bashes. I met Harmon at one of them. He tried to recruit me for the Network, but that did not appeal to me. Maybe, I became a challenge for him. He spent a great deal of time with me and we fell in love. He is, rather he was, an interesting and entertaining man. He made no secret that he was married, although he did not love his wife. I was sure of that. She didn't even have any interest in the children, while he worshiped them. Having the children would have been fine with me just as long as I had him. She agreed to give him a divorce but demanded $200,000 for full custody of the children." She paused to take a sip of her coffee. "His business had been dropping off and he had borrowed against it to the hilt. His parents had forfeited all of the money they made from the Network, including the part that was supposed to go to him. My father would never have forked over that kind of money, and when I told him I was going to marry Harmon he, of course, had him investigated and would never condone a marriage to a man whose parents were convicts. I went to work for him as his personal secretary so we could be together and work things out." The maid interrupted as she brought in a second round of coffee. "It was Harmon's mother who came up with the blackmail scheme to get the money. One of the reasons there were no records of the Network was because Pauline had a photogenic mind and could remember every detail. She knew every real name of all of the Network women spread out across the country. From there it was easy to track down those who had emerged to a position for easy prey to blackmail for the secret about their haunting past. She could do nothing from prison, but Harmon could handle it all from the outside. If my father knew he would kill me, but I was willing to become a criminal to help him. Harmon even predicted that the Wharton woman would seek you out to avoid notoriety and that when the time was right he would be able to convince you that this would be a one-time matter, and that everyone would then be able to live happy ever after. Who would figure that his wife would go bonkers and kill him? That night she stormed into the office and found us making love on the sofa. She started screaming and carrying on. She pulled a gun out. I think she was aiming at me and tried twice. Both times it hit Harmon. Then she bolted out of there. I panicked, just envisioning my father reading the headlines if I got involved in this. So, I ran out, hoping against hope not to get involved. I was completely shaken. I truly loved him, and to this day I miss him and cry for him. That's it. End of story. End of crime. The blackmailer is dead and the need for the money is gone with him. We can all return to our petty lives and you emerge as the hero who saved the day. Nobody has really been hurt except Harmon, me, and his mother."

She recrossed her legs and a tear slid down her cheek. It was as if a stream was flowing over fine sand. He bought her story but not her conclusion. "It's not as simple as all that. Anguish causes damage and anticipation can be hurtful. And, what about the new note?"

Her azure eyes opened wide, and he figured she was truly surprised. "What new note?"

"The new blackmail note."

Her voice raised to the level of her anger. "There is no new note. There can't be!"

"Well, there is."

Her tone lowered but not the gist of her frustration. "Then, it is something new and different. It's not from me or Pauline."

"How do I know that?"

"There's no reason, no incentive."

"It is a lot of money. Temptation comes easily in such a picture. And, how am I to be assured there never will be more notes?"

"You and they will just have to believe that."

"So, who is behind the new note?"

She squirmed in her seat. "Beats me!"

"It mentions the earlier ones."

She seemed genuinely shocked. "Can't be!"

"It's true. Who else could have gotten wind of this?"

"I don't see how."

"What about someone else at the agency?"

"No way. We were careful, very careful to keep it to ourselves."

"Then you explain to me how we got from there to here."

She stood and paced back and forth quickly. There was utter grace in every movement. "I don't know. I really have no idea how it could be."

He believed her, and he also believed that she had lost the man she loved, a man she would have defied her father to have and keep. He knew what that kind of love was. He could be hard on her, but there was no point to it. His voice softened, and he was surprised that he could feel sympathy for anyone besides himself. "What are your plans now?"

She sat, crossed those perfect legs, and watched him drain the second mug of coffee. "I don't know. I have disappointed my parents and brothers, so I do not feel comfortable here. At this point I have no place to go to, no place I want to go to. San Francisco would be the last place. I suppose given time I will figure something out."

"You are young and beautiful, and I know you are smart. Your whole life is ahead of you. Take it from one who knows, don't waste it."

"Will there be any trouble from you or the ladies?"

"Not if you have been truthful. If you think of who might have picked up on this, you need to let me know." He handed her a piece of paper with his cell phone number on it.

"I will. I certainly will."

As the front door closed behind him, he had the sense he was back in the original Network case. There were no leads, and he had no idea where to look next. He either had too much coffee or not enough coffee to fix on what he had overlooked.

FOURTEEN

Len was stymied as well. While discussing it with Howard, the way he looked at it was that as careful as Harmon and Darby thought they had been, someone at the travel agency knew about it, or someone close to Grace or Norma had seen the notes, or somehow the notes were seen in transit. The overt weakness in these scenarios was that the new blackmailer would not really know what the blackmail was about. Sure, he or she or they might just be riding on the crest of the blackmail threat and counting on not having to disclose anything which would show the lack of knowledge. That just seemed too unlikely, even if the risk was deemed worth taking. After all, $100,000 from each lady is a whole bunch of money.

Howard was fairly certain that when Pauline got out of prison the desire for money would make the blackmail scheme irresistible. Pauline was high class, and that brought with it the expectation of a life style that required lots of money. He doubted she would try again with Grace or Norma because she would be readily connected to that. But, she knew the names of all the women who were trying to protect the Network secret, and some of them would have risen to some position of prominence by the prison release date. She would figure some way to capitalize on that vulnerability. Such a future scenario was not Howard's immediate concern. That would be for another time, another place, and another sleuth.

Norma received a note similar to the one Grace had. Since she knew it was coming, her reaction was more of exasperation than anything else.

Howard would hate for Grace to have to raise the money, but at this point the only thing he could think of was to lay an elaborate trap once the blackmailer conveyed the instructions for delivery of the money. Howard was fairly certain that the blackmailer did not have concrete proof of the ladies' network secret past, but just the allegations would be sufficient to produce enough of a negative innuendo to ruin Grace and Norma's careers. It was all so tenuous that he started to have serious doubts about what he was doing. The other unknown was what the new blackmailer might be capable of. It was unlikely that Harmon would have used force or done anything of a violent nature against the women. Now, even that was up in the air. If it was a possibility, how would he be able to protect them? It all just seemed to make it more imperative to catch the blackmailer now.

It had been a busy morning at the gun shop, and by the middle of the day he told the owner he was going to the back room to nurse a cold coffee and take a nap. He was tired in all three of the vital ways – physically, mentally, and emotionally. Little did he know he was about to be pressed to the limit.

There was a timid knock on the closed door. Opening the door, the person standing there was probably the last person he expected to see, other than Alice. Len came in and closed the door behind him. "I'm glad you are alone."

Bleary eyes could not obscure the serious look on Len's face. "Is something wrong?"

Len sat across the table from him. "Yes, everything is wrong."

"Joan and the children O.K.?"

"Yes and no."

"For as long as I have known you, you love to talk in riddles."

"I have a confession to make." He looked down at the table and then directly into Howard's eyes. "We have worked together and been friends for a long time. You know me better than anyone else, even better than Joan." His eyes closed and then sprang open. "I am the blackmailer! At least, I have tried to be the blackmailer. I can't go through with it."

The shock added to his already depleted condition made Howard utterly speechless. Len continued as if Howard had actually encouraged him to say more. "I suppose it is all well and good to be the sheriff of a small town. It is nice I'm given a house to live in. But, the salary above that is very meager and it is ten years before I can get Social Security, and even that will be minimal. When Joan and I got married, we talked about traveling to see the world. She was so excited about the prospect, but has not dared bring it up since then knowing it is impossible. There is no money to send the children to college, and I cry thinking about them being straddled with student loans for much of their lives. Parting with that money would not have been a hardship for the ladies, but it could do so much for me and the family. Yet, I can't live with myself to do this as easy as it is. The law is my religion, and I just can't carry out what I know is wrong no matter how much the incentive to do otherwise. It is a poor and tormenting legacy I am going to leave behind me. My respect and admiration for you has bolstered my backing down."

Everything solved in the swoop of a declaration. All of Howard's concerns and newly established frustration evaporated into thin air. Then, why was he not elated? Once again, believing his capacity to feel was gone reality proved otherwise. His heart swelled with pity for his friend. If he was in Len's shoes he too would have been tempted to bow to expediency. How much he must have agonized through all of this! "Len, I really don't know what to say."

"You don't have to say anything," Len responded in a hoarse whisper.

"I feel I must.   We have been through so much together. I don't want you to be alone in this decision.   I am proud to be your friend, and I am envious that you have the strength to make it right."

"Funny you should say that.   I call it a weakness."

"No, you will never regret it.   Even if it had all gone the way you hoped it would, you would never be able to live with yourself. I know from what I say.   I can't live with myself as I feel responsible for what happened to Alice.   Losing her has left me a shell of a man. And, what if you had wound up in prison?   Where would the family be then?   Could you do that to them?   You have a calm life, secure in a limited way.   You can look in the mirror without flinching."

"Will this be just between us?"

"You can count on that."

"I feel better.   My dear friend, I owe much to you."

They shook hands and then hugged.   After Len left, Howard felt strangely refreshed.   Alice would have approved of his reaction.

FIFTEEN

Grace and Norma were so relieved to know that it was over that they did not give vent to their curiosity by asking him for details. Both knew they avoided the conflict that might have been faced if the blackmailer was actually caught. They would have to press charges if there was interest in punishment for the crime. Most likely in that process the secret they so much wanted to protect would have become known. So, perhaps, Darby's pronouncement that everybody could now live happily ever after could be the result. The only problem with that is that life is a four-letter word, and in real life there is rarely a happily ever after.

Now that it was apparently over, Howard slipped back to the existence he sentenced himself to. Day merged into day, week into week. Waning energy led him to lose concentration and direction, and if he was not dead already he could not escape the notion he was dying.

It was late morning at the gun shop, and the third coffee had no taste at all. He drank it more from habit than for enjoyment. Just when he was starting to think that he could use a good dose of sultry, Grace came through the door with a sandwich bag and two paper cups of coffee. She did not smile and did not say anything. She just pointed in the direction of the back room. Even in his beleaguered condition he knew that was not a good sign.

Once inside, she pulled out a turkey sandwich from the bag and gave him half. She opened his coffee and placed it before him.

She did not sit.   After sipping some coffee, the sultry voice was still there but it was not as powerful as he recalled it to be. "The other half of the sandwich is for you for later.   I am too upset to eat. I need your help again."

There was still enough sultriness to subdue his denial mode. Howard guessed this was some form of black magic. "I'm not sure I am up to it."

"You are and you will be. You are the only one who can."

He was far from sure that such confidence was justifiable, but he was not going to fight it. "I guess that is decided."

"Yes, it is. I am sending you on a trip."

It almost sounded like a medical remedy. "Where to?"

"North Carolina.   Every Representative has a district office. Mainly, it is a token place for constituents to go to mostly for complaints. Anyway, mine is in the small burg I lived in, Manly, North Carolina, with a population of less than four hundred.   I cared for my mother there.   My mother's best friend, Rose Allanti, who took care of her in my absence and was of great help when I went back, works the office for me.   She is the only one there.   It once was a gas station, and even still has the pump stands in front. She lives in a house less than a half mile down the road so she can walk to the office. It is open four hours a day two days a week and by appointment. Rose is a good natured woman, has a heart of gold, and wouldn't hurt a flea.   I am very fond of her, and trust her implicitly. I don't want anything to happen to her.   Here is the note I received yesterday."

Howard unfolded the sheet of paper. Cut out letters from a newspaper were used to form the words and then pasted to the sheet of paper.

RESIGN OR ROSE
WILL BE HURT BAD

Grace took the note back and continued. "I want you there to protect her. I just have a feeling this note comes from there, too. Most likely, only the locals know Rose by name. Doesn't sound to me like money is going to be involved."

He had to agree with that. "I think you have me mixed up with superman."

She half-smiled. "Aren't you?"

"A professional body guard might be your ticket."

"You're my man for the right reasons. Rose does not know about this and I want to spare her from any distress. She knows you are coming for awhile supposedly to work on a special project for me that I don't want anyone to know about. She has a small furnished apartment above her garage that I am renting for you, and she will feed you. She is Italian and a great cook. I hope you like lots of garlic. I told her to buy a very large coffee pot."

"Are you sure this is the way you want to handle it?"

"I wouldn't be here if I wasn't. Same contact arrangement. Same money. Hopefully, same success."

She was gone as quickly as she came. Time to splash cold water on the face he hated to face. He traded his last two weeks wages for a handgun and took a leave of absence from the store. He gave his landlord a month's rent in advance and was glad he had gotten a better car before moving to D.C.

He headed for North Carolina with absolutely no idea what he was getting himself involved in. The one consuming reality he would have to meet head on was that he had failed to protect Alice. What made him think, much less be capable of, protecting Rose? The stark difference was that he did not think Alice was in peril. He knew Rose was in danger. Perhaps, the last vestige of his being was riding on this task. Failure would undo him entirely. Success might be some form of redemption, but even if it was what good would it do? It was not as if he had a life to hold on to. His life was lost and beyond saving, but he could try his best to save the life of another.

SIXTEEN

The town sure was small. Howard had no trouble finding Grace's office, which was closed, and then the short distance to Rose's house. He pulled up at the house besides an old blue automobile which he assumed belonged to Rose. It was a warm early May day and two women were sitting in rockers on the porch. As he approached the steps leading up to the porch, his trained eye noted that one of the ladies was middle-aged and overweight with straggly hair that was nearly all gray. The other woman appeared to be about the same age, but she was thin, almost too thin, with long brown hair flecked with gray. It did not take a master detective to determine that the second lady was blind. A narrow face had massive scar tissue around her eyes and a blind person's cane rested against the wall by the rocker. "Good afternoon, ladies," he said as cheerfully as he was able to.

The chubby woman spoke up in a soft voice, "Whatever you're selling we don't need it or want it."

"That's no way to greet a visitor who traveled a spell to get here."

"Mr. Jensen?"

"Yup. Are you Rose?"

"I am Rose, and this is my sister, Violet."

"Howdy, Violet. Please call me Howard. I don't take a hankering to Mr. Jensen."

"Come and sit a spell, Howard. It's a perfect day. I'd make you some coffee but I see you have some. Grace had me order a large new pot."

"It is my staple." He sat in a vacant rocker. "Violet, are you visiting?"

Violet chuckled, thin lips parting to show straight white teeth in contrast to the scars on her face. Her voice was even softer than Rose's, barely audible over the sound of the rockers doing their thing. "No. I live here."

Howard grimaced as he tried to digest that piece of information. There were two women he had to look out for. "That's nice," was about all he could say.

"There is a third sister," Rose offered. "Can you guess her name?"

"Does she live here, too?"

"No, she is upstate."

"Well, you both were named after flowers, so I would hazard a guess that her name is Daisy."

"Not quite, but close. Her name is Iris. Howard, you should have been a detective."

"Maybe, so. Sure is quiet here compared to Washington. I am not going to miss the sound of traffic, airplanes, and sirens."

Rose was definitely the more talkative one. "Should be. The town has been dead for over twenty years, ever since the shoe factory closed. Most of the folks worked there, including us. When it closed, the smart ones moved away to find new jobs. We were sort of stuck here. Some years before the shut down, one of the leather dye vats exploded and poor Violet who was close by at the time was splattered with the stuff in her eyes. The company paid her until they closed, and now she gets a small social security disability amount, not enough worth mentioning. She stays mostly in or by the house. She knows every inch of the inside so she can get around real well without the cane. We eat supper at 5:00 and breakfast at 7:30. You are on your own for lunch. The only eating place in town is Simpson's down on Main."

"Two meals a day is more than I am used to. I survive on coffee."

"So Grace says. She told me to get that extra large pot and I'll have it going for both meals. I hope you like it black because sugar and milk are in short supply."

"Black is the only way. It has already stunted my growth. I used to be over six feet tall."

Violet laughed. "I think that is a tall tale."

"For someone who can't see, you see right through me."

Rose continued as if there had been no sidetrack to the conversation. "Grace has paid for everything, so she must expect great things from you. I can help you if you need anything."

"Thanks, I'll keep that in mind." He was sure she was being polite and trying to be helpful, but she might have been a bit curious and was hoping he would mention what he would be working on. Grace thought highly of her, and she seemed quite sincere, so there was really no need to question her motives.

The apartment over the garage was small but certainly adequate for his limited needs. The furniture was old and the bed lumpy, but it was clean and a better accommodation than what he had in Washington. One side window gave him a good view of the house, and from the other side window he looked down and could plainly see the office. There were few trees, so it was a good vantage point on both fronts. There was another house just over a ridge, but it did not seem menacing.

After unpacking his few things, he lay down to rest his weary eyes and body. It would be an hour before supper, and he dozed fitfully. No rest was ever peaceful. It was more of an interlude between pangs of guilt and remorse.

Grace sure was right about Rose being a good cook. Howard enjoyed every morsel, and complimented her frequently. Even the coffee was wonderful, and if he did not have a serious mission this could be a vacation of a lifetime for a man with a broken heart and a tortured spirit. Violet did not say much but she was attentive. Rose made up for the lack of conversation, and by the time the meal was over, Howard knew a great deal about the town and its people as well as the opposing candidate who had his election office in the next county.

Back in the garage quarters, he figured he would go to the office with Rose the next day to get a feel for that place, and try to get to know her daily routine. Then, he would do the same for Violet. He would probably come off as a nosy person, but he believed strongly that if you do not know it you cannot deal with it.

SEVENTEEN

Howard reported to the sultry voice that he was here and there would be two to protect. Grace offered to double what she was paying him. He congratulated her on getting two for the price of one.

Sleep came in short spurts. Several times he got up and peered through the window at the house. He thought about going over to make sure that Rose locked the doors as he had advised her to do. He would leave that checking for other times. It was hoped that his car parked in the front might be a deterrent at least initially because whoever made the threats probably did not count on there being a visitor in Rose's life.

At breakfast, he lingered over a fourth cup of coffee after Rose left for the office. Violet was still at the table. Howard told Rose he would be to the office shortly, but as long as he had Violet by herself he would find out as much as he could about her daily activities. "Thanks for keeping me company, Violet."

"Howard," her voice was almost lyrical, "It is nice having someone to talk to. We don't get many visitors, and I think my hideous face scares away those who do come."

"Your face is not repulsive." He meant that. From what he could tell she had an overshadowing inner beauty.

"Maybe you are the one who is blind."

"I'm being truthful."

"You sound sincere, and because of my blindness I can tell

genuine expressions from lies. Yet, I know who I am. Long ago, I stopped feeling sorry for myself. There is no benefit in it. It just adds to the torment. I listen to music on the radio, classical music. I like to think my blindness allows me to appreciate more than a seeing person can. If I let the music filter into my soul I become the music. Just listen to me. I haven't talked this much since forever."

"It is a pleasure to listen to you."

"Flattery is not sincere."

"It is if it is meant to be." He was not going to say this but it came out anyway. "I feel sorry for myself. Perhaps, I can learn a thing or two from you."

"What is wrong? I have detected a sadness in your voice."

"At another time we can talk about it. I have bigger fish to fry at the moment."

"What is going on? What are you after?"

"I'm not after anything."

"You are a big city man making small talk with a blind country bumpkin."

"One who happens to be pleasant to talk to."

"Why are you here? I think blindness also makes me highly perceptive. There is more to this than what you have told us. I think you are harboring secrets."

He should make this woman a detective partner. "Is it that obvious?"

"To me, yes. After all, I have few distractions. I am in the house all of the time and other than the music and reading braille, I can concentrate on the emotions I sense."

He noticed the long thin fingers and figured with her love of music she could have been a musician herself in a different life. "I am starting to doubt you are blind. You see right through me. Do you tell Rose everything?"

She did not respond for a moment. "I have never had a reason not to tell her."

"And if I gave you a reason?"

"It would have to be a very good one."

He felt a half truth coming forth, a not-so-admirable detective's prerogative. "Grace does not want Rose to worry about anything. She feels there are some underhanded practices going on involving her reelection. I am a retired detective, and she sent me down here to see what is going on. She not only does not want Rose to worry, but she thinks if Rose knows about it she might act differently and thereby tip off anybody who might be involved."

"I wouldn't want Rose to worry about anything either. She is an angel of mercy. Not only does she care for me, but she took care of Grace's mother as well as many others around these parts who need a helping hand. She would have made a wonderful mother but that possibility disappeared with the shoe factory. You will soon discover there are few men here. In fact, you may not be safe from a bunch of eager females."

He grunted. "At my age and dilapidated condition, no woman would want me."

"Why, how old are you?"

"Fifty-seven going on eighty. I have never taken care of myself; don't eat right; and drink too much coffee."

"Your voice reveals a caring person, and I can tell you are smart."

"Nicest things anyone has ever said to me."

"While you are here, Rose and I will work on getting you together."

Howard thought to himself *How do you overcome an impossibility?* "Real nice of you."

"Anyway, I won't say anything to Rose. I now know why you are cautious and want us to lock the doors."

"Exactly."

"I won't be any help in what you are after. I am confined to the house not because I have to, but it is where I am most comfortable. I am afraid of people. Frankly, I don't like them because I know they stare at me, shake their heads in disbelief, and think I am a freak. I don't like to go to places I have not been to before. But, if I can do anything to help you, just ask."

"Mighty kind of you." Behind the scar tissue and beyond the far too thin body there existed a beautiful person. He was sure of that. He had an urge to hug her, but he was unable to do anything like that. He wondered if Alice would mind if he embraced another person in his shattered heart.

Rose was hunched over the computer when Howard entered the office. She looked at the coffee cup he had in his hand. "Do I need to get a pot for the office?"

"No. I really need to cut back, although I can't change fate."

"Having less coffee is not fate. It is a health decision."

"I can't escape the fact, and I call it fate, that it keeps me going."

"Well, we'll just have to come up with something else that will keep you going."

"Good luck with that. I'll make sure I get the cup back to the house."

"Grace sends me emails all the time. She says that you might ask me to do some things that don't make sense and I should just do them. I should tell her I now lock the doors. I am sure she will get a laugh out of that. I also register every constituent request and complaint. This is a busy month. There have been two complaints already."

"What's the most you have gotten in a month?"

"Five."

"Are there any repeat complainers?"

"One each month is the same person."

"Who is that?"

"Shirley Wilson. Nothing makes her happy."

"What does she complain about?"

"Anything and everything. Congress fails to do this or that and needs to do this or that."

"Any complaints about Grace personally?"

"Yeah. There is a history between the two that I never got all of the details. They were in high school together and were friends until something happened between them. Now, her biggest complaint is that Grace should be here more often. You would think that she would want her to stay away. But, that is probably the worst thing she can come up with. Why do you want to know all this?"

"Just to get the big picture. What does Shirley do?"

"She works the counter at Simpson's."

"I'll take a walk downtown and maybe stop there for some coffee."

"I thought you said you were cutting back."

"I would suffer serious withdrawal symptoms."

"You really should."

"You're right."

"Do you need to use the computer for anything?"

"Don't know the first thing about computers. I am not cyber literate. I am not sure I belong in the modern world."

Rose was serious. "I don't think you are missing out on anything." She reached into a drawer of the desk. "Here is a key in case you want to come here while I am elsewhere. Actually, I have to leave shortly to get the car. I'll take the cup back to the house. I need to go to Sam's farm a few miles out of town. His wife has been sick. I am taking the leftovers from supper, and I'll keep her company for a spell. When I was young, I wanted to be a nurse. The shoe factory was the only real choice, but I still feel best when I look after others. I love to cook and eat, as you can tell. Violet eats like a bird, that is why she is skin and bones. There is usually someone out there who can use the leftovers. Of course, I wasn't always fat. Violet is the one who had the best shape. She was engaged when the accident happened, but he turned out to be a scoundrel and dumped her when he saw her afterwards. I can't stand cruel people!"

"You're one nice person, Rose."

"Is there any other way to be?"

Howard wondered if she had been talking to Vicky. "A lot of people believe so."

"Shame on them."

Only here a day, and Howard was already fond of Rose and Violet and concerned about them. He just could not let anything happen to them.

EIGHTEEN

Downtown was a misnomer. There was no town for a down. Among a bunch of empty, dilapidated stores, there was one general store and a rundown restaurant with a handmade sign reading Simpson's. At the end was a somewhat larger abandoned building that had etched in the cement over the front door Town Hall. It was boarded up as were the empty stores. The only vehicles on the street were two older trucks and a beat up sedan parked by Simpson's.

Gringy at dingy. Could be a horror story title or an apt description of Simpson's. It sure must have seen better days, and everything seemed well outdated particularly by Washington D.C. standards. Howard was not sure he would actually eat in a place like this but he had some bad coffee over the years so he would chance that. Two older men were sitting at a table off to the side. It was before the lunch hour so maybe there might be more people there later on. Not likely, but what did he know?

He sat at the counter. The chair still swiveled, so that was a good sign. A woman came out of the kitchen. Her pink uniform was wrinkled although clean. Perhaps, he had encountered his counterpart at the counter. The woman was about Grace's age but quite a contrast in appearance. She was not attractive and was stocky and with muscular arms protruding from the short sleeves of the uniform. Unkempt brown hair fell over ears with large earrings dangling down. Her skin was tough looking, a far cry from Grace's soft skin. If this was Shirley, Howard would guess that she was and probably had always been envious of Grace. That easily could have been part of the fallout in the high school days.

The voice was not sultry either. In fact, it had a harshness to it that might have made him order too much or too little. "Hey there, stranger."

"Hey there, yourself."

"Passing through?"

"No, visiting."

"Never seen ya before. Who ya visiting?"

Howard figured he better not say anything about Grace. If this was Shirley, and he was fairly certain she was, she would either clam up or bite his head off. "Violet Allanti."

That took her by surprise. "Didn't know Vi had any friends."

"Yeah. We go way back."

"What's ya name?"

"Howard. What's yours?"

"Shirley. Ya have a last name?"

"I do."

She snapped at him. "What is it?"

"Can I get some coffee first?"

She filled an earthen mug from a silex pot that barely had a cups' worth of coffee in it. It might have been sitting there since early morning or for even days. After placing it before him, she sputtered, "I hope ya like it black. There's no milk or sugar. No clean spoons out of the kitchen yet."

"Black will do."

"And, the name?"

"Jensen. Yours?"

"Don't ring a bell. Wilson. How do ya know Vi?"

"I'm a salesman in the braille book business. Violet has been a customer for a long time, and we became good friends along the way."

"She's a loner. Didn't think she knew a soul. Her sister is a busy body. Ya probably know she works for Grace?"

The coffee was strong but not as bad as some he had. "I know that."

"Do ya know she is a bitch?"

"I thought she was a congresswoman?"

"A wise guy, eh? Grace is supposed to represent us but looks out for nobody but herself."

"That's not what I read about her."

Shirley patted down her stringy lifeless brown hair. "Blown out of proportion. Ya can read whatever, we know the truth here."

"I gather you didn't vote for her?"

"Not in a million years! She only won cause she made some way out promises she has no way of keeping."

"Like what?"

"Ya ask a lot of questions for a book salesman."

"That's what salesmen do."

"Well, I don't discuss politics with strangers."

Howard thought it would be best if he changed the subject for now. "How long have you lived here?"

"All my life."

"I bet it was a real nice town at one time."

"Long ago, maybe. If a bunch of terrorists came here and blew it away, nobody would miss it."

"So, why do you stay?"

"Good question, salesman. One reason I stay is to vote Grace out of office. The other reasons I don't discuss with strangers."

"Seems like you don't like her?"

"That obvious? I hate her."

"She can't be that bad."

"She is and some."

"Who is running against her?"

"Fred Belknap, over in Aimsbury."

"Is he any better?"

"No comparison. He has it all together."

"I'll have to meet him."

"His campaign office is in Aimsbury. He is also the sheriff there so he is around."

That was interesting information. Howard was pretty sure he had his first two suspects.

NINETEEN

At supper, it was not lost on Howard that Violet had changed from baggy slacks and a sweatshirt to a dress. Her hair was combed back in a pony tail and she looked younger. Howard was sure that Rose noticed it as well because she smiled each time she looked over at her sister.

Once involved with eating, Howard related his conversation with Shirley. "She doesn't like Grace, not one little bit."

"Yup," Rose interjected. "There are a few folks like that."

That was not what Howard wanted to hear. Another old detective's prophecy is that the more suspects the less certainty. "Who else votes against her with such a strong feeling?"

"Two that come right to mind are Tonya Herbert and Wilma Frazier."

"What's their squabble?"

"Tonya raises chickens, and one of the first pieces of legislation that Grace backed was for stricter agricultural inspections, including on chicken breeders. Wilma and Grace had a spat some years back. I can't remember what it was about, but Wilma has carried a grudge ever since."

"What about Fred Belknap?"

"He's the other party candidate. Ran against her last time, too. He lost by a few votes so he is sore about that. He is the sheriff in Ames county, and everyone knows he is inept. That is why he lost. He'll lose again by more this time unless a miracle comes his way."

Howard could put that in context. "I think I'll have a talk with him."

"Don't count on him being cooperative, especially if he knows you are working for Grace. He won't give me the right time of day."

With a full belly, Howard carried a cup of coffee out to the front porch. Violet was in a rocker and he sat in an adjoining one. Rose was in the kitchen cleaning up. He looked over at Violet and thought she would be particularly beautiful if she put on some weight. The scar tissue around her eyes was barely noticeable to a man who had seen much worse. Visions of Alice on the bed flashed in his mind as well as the other victims of the Network. "Nice night, isn't it Violet?"

"It is. Can you hear the crickets?"

"Now I do. At times, things have to be pointed out to me."

"Your voice is still sad."

"Probably always will be."

"Want to tell me about it?"

"I don't want to depress you or for you to feel sorry for me."

"I told you I no longer feel sorry for myself. Perhaps, I can share in your pain and that way it will be less for you."

Yes, Violet was one beautiful person. "Your kindness is appreciated, very appreciated. I will spare you the details. After a loveless life, I finally met a woman I loved and who loved me. Before we could enjoy any life together, she was murdered by some of the same people involved in a case I had been working on. She was killed to get back at me. It sapped the last life out of me. I just function on the outskirts of an existence."

Violet reached out her hand and it touched his arm. The long slender fingers clutched at his shirt sleeve. "Tragedies come in many different packages. I understand your agony, and I hope I can make you feel you are not alone in this. I was in love once, before the accident. He disappointed me by rejecting me when he saw what it had done to me.   That hurt as much as the chemicals going on my face and in my eyes.   For the longest time I could not understand how love could not override a change in appearance when the person was basically the same.   Finally, I rose above it by telling myself that because of his reaction he was not worthy of my love.   Loneliness also comes in many forms.   I am lonely knowing I have a great capacity to love a man but there is no man to love.   I bear the loneliness not as a form of punishment but as a type of reality I need to accept or be miserable.   I try to be happy. Music has helped me a great deal. I know it's not easy, Howard, but try to learn from me.   Keep the warm memories in your heart, and since you are in a position to help others make that your happiness."

Howard placed his callous hand over those magical fingers. "You are one wise woman. One day I may see what you mysteriously see in your blindness. Until then, the climb out of my hole is too difficult and I am not in condition to try it.   I do feel better talking to you about it.   There is more comfort in sharing misery than I imagined."

Rose came out on the porch and noticed Violet's hand on Howard's arm and his hand over her fingers.   She smiled and sat in a rocker. The chorus of crickets took it all in.

❖

TWENTY

The drive over to Aimsbury was revealing in its own way. He had seen a lot of squalor in D.C., but in some ways it appeared more pronounced here as he drove by dilapidated houses and an abundance of old mobile homes. Lawn areas were strewn with junk and garbage, and open areas were unsightly in their own way. It was not what one would expect in the country. The stark contrast between the rich and the poor in this nation was a constant reminder that society is out of kilt. Even as he surveyed his own life, finances were always a struggle and the battle was usually to think about fine things and to learn to do without them. It defied his comprehension how those without a job and hope managed at all. The more he thought about that, the more he could understand why Len was so tempted to carry out the blackmail scheme.

He tried Fred Belknap's campaign office first. It was locked and there was no sign of any activity. Asking at the gas station where the sheriff's office was, he tried that next. It was locked, and by all indications there had not been an open door for awhile. At the post office, he asked for directions to Fred's house.

Fred was not at his modest house either, although an official sheriff's vehicle was parked out front. His wife, Harriet, answered the knock on the door. She held back a fiercely barking dog as Howard explained that he wanted to talk to Fred. Harriet was tall and rather plain looking although friendly. She invited him in, locked up the dog, and made him coffee. Fred was down fishing at the creek but was expected back momentarily.

Howard was on his second cup of coffee and nibbling on one of Harriet's sugar cookies when Fred arrived. Fred was very tall, probably six feet and a half, slightly stooped at the shoulders, and while on the slim side he had a protruding beer belly. He was not in a sheriff's uniform but in old clothes most likely kept aside for fishing.

After introductions, Fred sat down at the table and joined him in a cup of coffee. Howard had decided on the drive over that a direct blunt approach would be best. Such might bring matters to a head quickly. "Well, Fred, I won't take up much of your time. I thought I had better meet you. I am now working with Rose at Grace Wharton's district office and I was hoping we could smooth out any rivalry so that we can all approach the upcoming election in a friendly fashion."

If Fred was surprised, he did not show it. "Mighty nice of you, really. I had my heart in the first election, but I am only running against her now because nobody else will. Frankly, I would be out of place in Washington. She knows it and I know it."

"I hear tell some are unhappy with her?"

"Ah, you can't please everybody. I know that just by being the sheriff."

"Do you have much crime here?"

"Some petty stuff. So little actually that I serve as sheriff for a bunch of counties. If anything serious happened, which would surprise the hell out of me, I'd have to call in the FBI."

"Have you seen Grace lately?"

"Haven't seen her since the last election when we both made speeches at the July 4th picnic. I was the first to admit her speech was better than mine. Didn't matter though. Folks had already decided. They were voting for me or against me. This time, they'll be voting for her."

Howard already had the sense that Fred, ordinary Fred, was not a suspect. The will was not there, and there was probably a lack of capability as well.

On the drive back, he thought more about Violet than who he would track down next. He could almost still sense her hand on his arm. He felt a rising affection towards her. It was the last thing he expected to experience. He was certain his heart was numb from the loss of Alice and that he could never feel that way about another woman. It was not pity because of her handicap or looks. It was also not an offshoot of self pity seeking a convenient release. More of a problem was that if she felt anything towards him was it something other than trying to lift his spirits?

When he arrived back at the house, Rose was in the kitchen preparing supper. Violet was in her room listening to music. He could hear it plainly, and even though he knew nothing about music he could see how relaxing it might be to listen to it. It would be nice to know more about it, especially if Violet did the explaining.

He went to the garage quarters and telephoned Grace. The sultry voice was reassuring, and he reported on his meetings with Shirley and Fred. He had concluded that Shirley was the prime suspect so far. He asked her what the story was with Wilma. Grace theorized that Wilma thought Grace had taken away a man from her that she thought was interested in her. Grace downplayed it saying it had all been in Wilma's imagination but over the years it had grown out of proportion. Howard knew all too well that facts produced by the imagination can be as powerful as the ones actually transpiring.

After supper, Howard asked Violet if she wanted to take a walk. She clung to his arm as they walked along the deserted road. The crickets were close by and a gentle breeze accompanied them. They walked in silence. It was just so pleasant being with her, he felt no need to say anything.

She stopped and turned towards him. In a low voice that

he barely heard she spoke as she moved closer to him. "Please hug me."

He enfolded his arms around her, very conscious of how thin she was. Her arms forcefully encased him, and they were that way for several minutes. "I am amazed that with Rose's cooking you are so thin."

"Eating is not a priority."

"What is?"

"Now, you. I want you to share the feelings I have for you."

"What is that?"

"An acceptance of who and what you are."

"I do that and more."

"Then, do you promise you will try to stop feeling sorry for yourself?"

"I will try. Before you, there was no way. Now, we'll see."

He bent down and lightly kissed her lips, also thin. She kissed him back, and for the moment at least the memory of Alice did not obliterate all other things.

They walked slowly back to the house. Rose was waiting on the porch. All seemed right with the world.......for the moment.

TWENTY-ONE

On the next day, Howard went to see Tonya Herbert at her chicken farm. The overalls she was wearing did not totally hide a nice shape, although her ruddy complexion was a tip off of a harsh farm life. Her deep raspy voice indicated a person not used to being defied.

Tonya was in the front yard to her shack-like house pruning bushes. She kept working on the bushes the whole time he was talking to her. "Tonya, I am Howard Jensen. I am now working in Grace Wharton's district office."

She looked at him briefly but the look said what she was about to say. "Why?"

"I admire the work she is doing in Congress."

He did not think she intended to be humorous, but it came out that way. "You must be lonely."

"You don't approve of her efforts?"

"No, and I don't approve of her. She's supposed to be voting for things that help us, not hurt us. What happened to Rose?"

"Rose is in the office with me. Grace doesn't back things that help you?"

"Not as far as I know. There are a bunch of chicken farmers here, and because of her things are harder now for us."

"I'll make a point to look into that, and I'll speak to her. You do realize there is a whole nation that needs looking after?"

She snapped a branch off of a bush that did not appear to

need snapping. "I don 't give a rat's ass about that!"

"Rather selfish, don't you think?"

"Why should you care?"

"I'm here to care."

"Then tell her we're hurting here and she damn well better do something about it."

"That sounds threatening."

"My very existence is threatened. Why shouldn't hers?"

"Because that is not the way an orderly society works."

"Blah on that!"

"So, I guess we can't count on your vote?"

"Damn straight!"

"Is there anything I can do to change that?"

"Bump her off!" The words slid out of the corner of her mouth.

Taking that in, he did not respond right away. "A bit drastic, don't you think?"

She turned away from him and went into the house. He guessed he was dismissed. In spite of the harsh talk, he thought it was just letting off steam. She was definitely angry, but angry enough to do a criminal act? Who would take care of the chickens? Of course, his judgment of people over the years had been wrong before, maybe even more wrong than right, but he concluded that if she had bad acts seriously in mind she would have been more evasive. He would put her on the maybe list.

Back at the house, he heard the music from Violet's room. Rose was out on one of her mercy visits that she had described at breakfast.

Howard knocked on Violet's closed door. "Come in, Howard."

He opened the door slowly, an act which would always be tinged with the memory of the time he opened Alice's bedroom door and found her slain. Violet was sitting at a small table with a braille book open before her. The music was orchestral, he could tell that much. She was dressed in jeans and a baggy sweater. "How did you know it was me?"

She smiled. "I can tell Rose's knock. Who else would it be?"

"You should be the detective."

She stood up and approached him, lifting her arms. He embraced her carefully. She tilted her face towards him, and as if it was the most natural act of his life he bent down and kissed her. "I liked that. Is it a detective's reward?"

"No. It is the reward for a gentle and caring woman."

Her smile was full and warm. "I can accept that."

"There's lots more where that came from."

She smiled again. "I certainly hope so."

❖

TWENTY-TWO

According to Wilma Frazier's neighbor, she was away visiting a cousin in Greensboro and it was not known when she would return. Howard's naturally suspicious mind vacillated between a legitimate trip and the creation of an alibi. The neighbor was not very talkative, except to tell Howard that Wilma pretty much kept to herself and that she made quilts. He did not have to be told about the quilts because there was a sign on the lawn in the front of the shack-like house that indicated quilts were for sale.

Rose could not think of anybody else who may have had a grudge or other form of animosity towards Grace. Howard looked through the records at the office, and that proved to be a waste of time and effort.

In order to maximize protecting Rose, Howard suggested he accompany her on the trips to deliver food and keep company with folks who were in need. He told her it would be a good way for him to get a feel for the community.

On a trip over to see a farmer's wife who had recently had a baby boy, Rose could not contain her inquisitiveness about the budding relationship with Violet. "Howard, I think you are a sincere person. I don't want Violet to be hurt."

"Believe me, I don't want her to be hurt."

"She has lived in a very small and sheltered world since the accident. She is vulnerable and starved for attention."

"I realize all of that. Actually, I feel Violet and I are very much alike. I live in a small and confined world as well. I think we are two lost souls."

"How are you a lost soul? You're a man of the world."

"I have told her of my misfortune. I had finally found love only to have her murdered because of me. It was a deliberate act to be as harmful as possible to me."

"I'm sorry, Howard. I truly am. I am not one to talk as my experience with people and relationships is nil, but I have to live with Violet after you leave and I can't handle an emotional breakdown. It has taken her a long time as it is to have reached a point of some form of contentment."

Not that he had thought it through, but at times hope overrides long consideration. "What if I was to tell you that I may not leave?"

She glanced sideways at him, a quizzical look on her face. "What are you saying?"

"I have no life to go back to. I am retired and work in a gun shop just to pass the time and subdue my memories for a time. After this assignment for Grace, I have nothing to do that I want to do. I have nobody I care about back there. I feel a strong emotional attachment to Violet. I probably need her more than she needs me, and I believe a mutual dependency would make us both stronger."

"And where do I fit in?"

"You are wonderful to and for her. Violet needs you as much as she needs me. I don't intend to come between you. I hope I would be an extra hand to help you both."

"Have you talked to Violet about all this?"

"I will."

"This is much for me to digest. I need to think about it and talk to her after you have said your piece."

"Sounds reasonable to me. I don't have much money, mainly just what Grace is paying me. I will apply early for Social Security."

"The house has been paid off a long time ago, so there are no great expenses. However, one never knows what emergencies, including medical ones, can change that,"

"I am a firm believer in handling things as they come along. Not very practical, for sure. I suppose I am accustomed to there being too many unexplained events to plan for them."

They reached the farm, and Howard sat on the porch drinking coffee for the two hours they were there. They were mainly silent on the way back. When all was said and done, he had not intended to make a commitment but he did. Was there enough of him left to see it through?

TWENTY-THREE

Howard's plan was to be seen as much as possible with Rose. Between that and his car parked out in front of the house, it might just be enough of a deterrent to ward off the carrying out of any violence. There was also the possibility that the threat had been an idle one and thrown out just to upset Grace.

It did not take long for that plan to collapse and for the idle threat theory to fly out the window. Two days later, Rose made a quick trip to a sick lady in the valley and Howard skipped going with her to be in the office to rearrange the furniture so that anyone looking in from the road could not see very much. Rose took the Old Mission Road back as it was a shortcut to the highway. Out of nowhere, a white truck came up behind her and nudged her car off the road and into a ditch and then sped off. Fortunately, the ditch was not deep at that point and since it had not rained for almost a week there was no mud in the ditch. Rose was able to keep control of the car and swerve back on to the road. It happened so fast and had taken her so completely by surprise that the only thing she noticed was the color of the truck. She was shaken up but did manage to drive back to the house. It took awhile for Howard and Violet to quiet her agitation.

Later, Howard asked her who had white trucks. Rose said she would have to think about it for awhile, although offhand the only one she could come up with was Wilma Frazier. She was emotionally tired, and right after cleaning up from supper she went to bed.

Violet hugged him for a long minute. "Howard, I am afraid.

Do you think someone wants to hurt Rose?"

"I certainly hope not. Yet, be extra careful. There are too many bad people out there, and while I don't want to frighten you any further we need to concentrate on ways to find out who they are and prevent them from doing anything harmful."

"How do I do that?"

He was not sure this was the right time for the talk he was hoping to have with her, but it was coming out anyway. "Not alone."

She hesitated as if she was afraid to say anything. "Rose is all I have."

He kissed her forehead. "Not any more. You now have me. If you will let me, I want to help Rose in looking after you."

She smiled and reached for his hand. "Blind people can see in their dreams. In my dreams I see you and me together. Is that silly?"

"No."

"When I was young, I thought love was as it was portrayed in the movies. I don't know what it is. Yet, I know when we are together I feel at ease. I am happy. Does that make sense? Do you feel that way?"

"Yes. I am as happy as I ever thought I could be again with you."

"You don't mind I am ugly?"

"Scars do not make ugly. They just mar what otherwise is perfection."

"You are the sweetest person I ever knew."

"Believe me, I surprise myself. You bring out in me the person I want to be but never was."

"If you will be my eyes, I will be your heart."

"I get the better part of the deal."

"Your voice no longer sounds sad."

"Nobody could be sad around you." He truly meant that.

"I want Rose to be part of this."

"She is and will be. She already knows how I feel."

"Does that mean you will stay with me?"

"I will if that is what you want."

"More than anything."

They kissed, and Howard made sure she was safely in her room before locking up and returning to the garage. His mind was as alert as it had ever been. Usually, a dead man's sleep would overtake him. Now, it was as if he had emerged from a long coma. He had a love with Alice, and it tragically ended before it could fully blossom. With Violet, it was as if he was given a second chance to do it all right. He swore to himself he would not fail this time.

TWENTY-FOUR

Before Howard could telephone Grace about the incident with Rose, she called him and told him she had received another note. This one said it was her final warning. Between the note and the actual attempt to injure Rose, Grace was quite upset. Howard tried to reassure her that he would bolster his vigil and that he thought Wilma might be the one responsible. Yet, without proof he did not want to confront her just yet. It seemed imperative that he make sure she had not gone to Greensboro or had come back already.

Rose did a computer search of the records of the Department of Motor Vehicles to see how many white trucks were registered in those counties comprising Grace's district. There were seventeen in addition to Wilma's. The only name that appeared to be of interest was Sam Belknap, who Rose said was Fred's brother. The only thing that Rose knew about Sam was that he worked at a lumber yard just outside of Aimsbury.

Before taking a drive over to the lumber yard, Howard swung by Wilma's house. There were no vehicles there and no visible signs that anyone had been in the house. The neighbor still had not seen her. Wilma and her truck were either away or she was one clever lady.

Sam's white truck was in the employee lot at the lumber yard. It was old and had a number of scrapes and dents. There were no blue marks, the color of Rose's car. Howard asked at the office for permission to speak with Sam Belknap and was directed out back. Sam was about the same height as his brother and more muscular. Howard guessed he was a younger brother. He was also not particularly friendly or talkative so Howard figured he better not tell him he was associated with Grace. He made up some story that he was working for an insurance company and trying to locate a white truck that had been involved in an accident on the turnpike. Sam insisted he was not involved and did not know anything about an accident and that he was at work at the time the accident was supposed to have happened. Howard verified that at the office. All in all, Howard would leave an opinion about Sam's connection open for the moment. He was probably not involved, but something just did not sit right about him. Maybe, it was just that Howard was wary of unfriendly people. He also had been suspicious of so many people and so many things over the years that it was ingrained in him. Violet, undoubtedly, would work on that about him along with everything else.

A couple of days later Howard went by Wilma's house. The white truck was parked on the side. It was also an older model and had various dents and scrapes. A quick look did not show any blue markings. He went to the door and, surprisingly, a beautiful woman opened the door. She was almost as attractive as Grace, and Howard could easily conceive a natural rivalry probably had existed between the two women. Her voice, however, was disappointing. There were no sultry tones, no softness in the expressions.

"Howdy," he smiled his best smile, "I'm interested in buying a quilt."

"Come in. You've come to the right place."

"I am Howard Jensen."

"Wilma Frazier. What size are you interested in?"

"Something small."

Apparently that did not sit right with her, and he determined that she had a basic suspicious nature just as he had. "What do you really want, mister?"

"I am sorry if I am frightening you. I am really here for some information with absolutely no evil purpose in mind. I am now working in Grace Wharton's district office and I am trying to help her in the reelection by making peace with those who object to her. I understand the two of you are on the outs. I figured if I said this right out you wouldn't talk to me."

Wilma chuckled. "Boy, she must be desperate for votes. I just came back from out-of-town and not even unpacked yet. Sit down and I'll give you an ear full. Can I get you a glass of water?"

"Kind of you. A cup of black coffee would be most appreciated."

"I don't drink coffee, so no pot. Instant coffee will have to do."

"Fine. Thanks."

"I can only imagine what you may have heard. None of it is true, and I actually voted for Grace. Let me get your coffee and then I'll tell you the story, the short version and still try to have you buy a quilt."

The room was small and the kitchen just off to the side. Howard already had a good feeling about this woman even if she was not a coffee drinker and had a white truck.

Wilma motioned for him to sit at the small table while she prepared the coffee. She then sat across from him as he began to drink. "Well, Howard Jensen, you don't seem like the type to be interested in a Hallmark movie type story, although my tale involving Grace is steeped in romance and broken hearts. I'll spare you the details, many of which I have long since forgotten anyway. Strange, isn't it, that things which seemed so important at the time lose their impact with the passage of time? Anyway, in high school, we were both interested in Guy Underfeld. Grace had always been prettier and more popular than me, so it really was no contest. I was a sore loser though.   There was no way we could be friends and we had nothing to do with each other.   Over the years, it all started to be so unimportant, and I wished we could have been friends.   Now, I admire her so much, and there was no way I could vote for Fred Belknap."

"How long have you had your truck?"

"It was my second husband's truck.   I have had it since we divorced six years ago.   I have had more luck with vehicles than with men.   Do you want to borrow it?"

"No, I was just curious I guess about a woman owning a truck."

"If you know Grace, you know better than to stereotype a woman."

He smiled.   "You certainly are right about that.   I can't understand why men don't fall all over you."

"Believe it."

"Too bad I am too old for you."

"Too bad I'm now into vehicles and quilts and not men."

"So, Wilma, you don't hold anything against Grace?"

"What for?"

"How about Rose?"

"Rose is a sweetheart.   She has done many kindnesses for me over the years."

"So, we can count on your vote?"

"Vote, yes.   Don't ask me to do any campaigning."

He just had to buy a quilt from this nice lady.   In fact, it would be putting Grace's money to good use.   He bought two small quilts for Rose and Violet to put over their legs while in the rockers if a chill set in.   As for Wilma, she was not a suspect.   If he was wrong about that then the quilts surely were pulled over his head.

TWENTY-FIVE

Rose was grateful for his company on her jaunts. That was the only progress Howard was making. He wondered if and how he might make a connection between Shirley and a white truck. He had determined she owned the old green sedan he had seen parked by the restaurant. He would talk with her in a few days and perhaps something might slip out in the process.

In the mean time, he went over to Aimsbury planning to ask Fred Belknap what he knew about people who had a white truck. If he mentioned his brother Sam, that would indicate a cooperative spirit. Fred was not at the campaign office or at the sheriff's office, so Howard went over to his house. The sheriff's car was parked in front. Harriet told him that Fred had gone down about a half hour earlier to fish in the creek. If he wanted to go see him, there was an easy half mile path down to the creek. Howard decided to do that, but Harriet offered him some coffee and an oatmeal raisin cookie she had baked earlier in the day. That took priority over talking to Fred for the moment. And, it turned out to be the best choice he had made in a long time. While chatting during the coffee and cookie indulgence, Harriet mentioned that Fred hated driving around in that conspicuous sheriff's car and would often go over to the lumber yard, leave the sheriff's car there, and borrow his brother's truck. He did that so often that he had his own key.

Even a rookie detective would not have to be beaten over the head with this kind of information to put two and two together. It all clicked, and Howard was on full scent. If a rattlesnake was on the path to the creek he would not have noticed it.

Fred was in high rubber boots midway in the creek. Howard decided to push the inevitable. "Hey, Fred, I have a bone to pick with you." His voice was so loud a thrush flew out of a bush on the other bank.

Fred turned directly towards him. "What's that? You scared the fish away."

"That's not all I'm going to scare." He placed his hand over the gun tucked in his pants beneath his jacket. "Rose was run off the road and recognized you in the truck that did it."

Fred's hesitation spoke volumes. Howard had experienced it many times in the past that a person's silence is tantamount to a verbal confession. "She must be mistaken. I don't have a white truck."

"I didn't say the truck was white."

"I thought you did. I still don't have one."

"Sam does."

Fred walked slowly out of the water and sat on a large rock. "I hated doing that." His voice did sound remorseful. "I like Rose. I made sure when I bumped her car that it was on that part of the road where the ditch was shallow. It was unlikely she would tip over and could easily gain control over the car. I bumped her as gently as I could so I probably didn't even damage her car."

"You've been sending threatening notes to Grace, too."

He stared at the ground. "I didn't like doing that either."

"Both are crimes. Rose could have panicked and totally lost control of the car and might have been hurt or even killed. That action as well as the notes are serious crimes, you of all people should know that."

"I do know that." He looked at Howard intently with pleading eyes. "Let me explain it all."

"I wish you would, and you better make it believable. There is no way to forgive a man to break the law he has sworn to uphold."

"Maybe yes, maybe no. Hear me out."

"Go ahead."

"What I told you about not wanting to be in Congress is true. But, call it pride or whatever, I just could not stand losing to a woman. People constantly rubbing that in hasn't helped. I think my own wife thinks less of me because that happened. Anyway, I got this idea which I can see now was really crazy that if I could get her not to run again, the only possible people her party could consider running against me are both men. I would still lose, but it would be to a man."

"Idiotic, to say the least."

"I know, believe me." Fred was on the verge of tears. "Please ask Rose and Grace to forgive me. I swear I will not do anything else. I will withdraw my candidacy, and there is no one else who will take my place to run against Grace."

"I'll tell her, but there is no way to know what she will do about this."

As soon as Howard was back in his car, he telephoned Grace. Relief overshadowed her bewilderment. She and Howard knew she was not going to do anything officially about it. The less publicity, the less involvement under all of the circumstances was best. The practical reality was that she would be running unopposed. As she so aptly put it, "I am now able to concentrate all of my attention and energy to my agenda to do the needed and great things for this nation."

Howard once again had to admit that sultry can be powerful. It can also be very loving. She added just before hanging up, "Howard, once again I thank you so much. I am putting you on the payroll and you can help Rose in the office however and whenever. Who knows, and I hope not, but I may need your special talent again. I am also glad you may have found some personal happiness there. Rose told me Violet loves you. Happiness has been a long time coming. You deserve it all, my friend."

He drove back to the house, back to Violet and Rose. His spirits were uplifted and his outlook brighter than it had ever been. In fact, he felt reborn. He might even give up coffee. Well, he was not quite that reborn.

www.ingramcontent.com/pod-product-compliance
Lightning Source LLC
Chambersburg PA
CBHW031840170626
46807CB00004B/1553